Showing Horses and Ponies

FRONTISPIECE   Seabrook, owned by Mr G. Buckingham-Bawden, winning the 1984
Show Hunter of the Year at Wembley.

Robert Oliver

Showing Horses and Ponies

Illustrated by Bob Langrish

PELHAM BOOKS

LONDON

First published in Great Britain by
Pelham Books Ltd
44 Bedford Square
London WC1B 3DP
1985

British Library Cataloguing in Publication Data

Oliver, Robert
Showing horses and ponies.
1. Horses——Showing
I. Title
636.1′0888   SF294.5

ISBN 0 7207 1582 2

Typeset and printed and bound by Butler & Tanner Ltd,
Frome and London

To the memory of
my great friend
Peter Reece

Contents

Preface

I have written this book with the intention of providing an interesting insight into the world of showing horses and ponies. I have assumed that the reader has some previous knowledge of horses and have not attempted to deal with the basic elements of horse management. Instead I have concentrated on those aspects of horsemanship which are relevant to the showman, be he novice or more seasoned competitor. For example, the health and welfare chapter is not intended to provide a comprehensive guide to equine ailments but rather serves to highlight problems of special relevance to the show animal.

I have dealt in the main with the show requirements of hunters, hacks, riding horses, cobs and show ponies. The book does not feature Mountain and Moorlands nor Arabs, Palaminos, Appaloosas, etc. as my knowledge does not extend to these breeds and I believe that you should only preach what you practise. Nevertheless, owners of these breeds will hopefully find the book otherwise useful.

In my chapter on heights and measuring I have endeavoured to explain how to measure correctly, as with a show horse an eighth of an inch either way can be the difference between a champion and an 'also ran', with thousands of pounds' value at stake.

The information conveyed in the pages that follow is based on the experiences and success that I have achieved over my years in the show ring. It must be remembered, however, that all the views expressed are my own and I would therefore ask the reader to bear this in mind when reading the book. Not everyone will agree with what I have to say but one cannot, after all, lay down hard-and-fast rules about horses as they are all individuals and need treating as such.

Many people outside of showing do not appreciate the work that goes into it and the enjoyment that can be had from owning and producing a show horse. It is a great art to produce a horse in absolute top show condition and still have it tranquil enough to behave in the modern show ring in the company of other horses. With all judging, exhibitors must remember that judges are not paid servants and that you exhibit your animal for their opinion. The judge's opinion is final and you must learn to accept defeat sportingly. It will be seen that animals are great levellers:

one day you are at the top and the next you are bottom. But there is always another day and another judge.

Showing is about the production of horses and ponies for the ring; showmanship is about attention to detail and presenting an animal so well that sometimes it will beat an animal with better conformation. This is where I hope this book will be of service.

Acknowledgments

I would like to take this opportunity to thank my many friends all over the world, especially those in England and Ireland, who have allowed me to ride and judge their horses. This I have tried to do sympathetically and to the best of my ability. Without the generosity and co-operation of these wonderful people this book could not exist.

Bob Langrish deserves a special mention for putting together the marvellous illustrations for the book, most of which were specially taken for the purpose. Other photographers to be thanked are: Kit Houghton (pp. 15 and 154), Monty (p. 127), Findlay Davidson (p. 68), J. Mayes (p. 150).

I am also grateful to those who have helped specifically with the preparation of this book, namely John and Sue Nelson and Christine Hughes.

Thanks, too, must go to my kind neighbours, the Biddlecombe and Garlick families, who so generously allow me to ride on their farms at Upleadon.

Finally, it would seem appropriate to mention here the splendid staff, past and present, who have worked so hard for me at Upper House Farm.

Robert Oliver
Upleadon
March 1985

1

Choosing a Show Horse or Pony

GENERAL CONSIDERATIONS

When assessing the show ring potential of any horse or pony natural balance and a level temperament, coupled of course with correct conformation are the most essential requirements. In addition a would-be champion should have that 'look of eagles' which makes him an equine aristocrat, both in his manners and in his appearance. This quality, 'presence', is the animal's hallmark of well-being; it is what catches the judge's eye and seems to say 'Look at me. I'm a champion.'

It is as well to consider that no matter how good your horse or pony is in its conformation, you still have to produce it for the ring. Later I will endeavour to explain how I think this can best be done.

When buying a show horse remember that he is only as valuable as his weakest point. No matter how good looking he is, if he has an unsoundness, regardless of how small, he can only be judged or valued accordingly. If a fault is very minor it may be detected only by the most experienced judge with the keenest eye. The more correct a horse's conformation the sounder he will be and consequently the longer he will last in any competitive sphere.

Quality in the show horse is difficult to define on paper and something which has to be seen to be appreciated. Presence, elegance and courage are just some of the recognisable qualities which exceptional show horses invariably possess. Whilst selecting a show horse do remember that the perfect horse has yet to be born. If his conformation is excellent he may fall short of requirements in his height or in the weight he is expected to carry.

The animal must be sound in its wind and make no noise at all, not even a whistle. Thus in hunter, hack or cob classes, if a judge, when riding an exhibit, hears anything he does not like he is entitled to place the animal at the bottom of the line, as, in his opinion, it is unsound. This also applies in pony judging but of course it is more difficult to detect a wind defect as the animals are not ridden by the judge.

Good faultless action is essential in the show animal. If the most correct looking animal cannot move really well it is heading for disappointment in the show ring. Although good basic schooling can improve a horse's action such an animal will always find itself at a disadvantage. In the hunter, good true straight movement with no signs of dishing is preferred to the more light and extravagant movement which is sought in the hack and pony. Movement should come from the shoulder and not from the elbow as the latter produces a stilted action. What one hopes to see is a markedly long and low movement with none of the knee action often seen in the more common horse or pony. With good movement one always has a smoother, more comfortable ride.

The more correctly made an animal is the easier it is to keep it in show condition, i.e. nicely covered in flesh and looking well throughout the season. A horse that is short backed and deep in the girth will always keep condition on whereas a long narrow animal will be a more difficult proposition.

In the successful show animal temperament is all important – even the most perfect animal will be greatly marred if mentally he is unsuited to the ring. The horse's outlook must suit his job, though of course the traits we hope to find vary from one purpose to another. For example, we look for courage in a hunter, and placidness in a small child's show pony. Highly strung animals are always difficult to show because the modern showground has so many distractions, e.g. displays, helicopters, etc.

I remember showing a novice small hunter at the Royal Show while hot-air balloons were floating overhead. The horse started to sweat and tremble, and failed to settle that day – in fact he never really settled again all season although at home and at small shows he was fine.

A hot gassy animal that requires hours of work before it will settle will never make a good show animal. Moreover, it will probably get worse as the season goes on. When going out to buy a show horse bear in mind that an animal with a level, placid temperament and a minor fault will take precedence over a world beater that is gassy and a hot ride.

Though colour is not really a point of conformation it makes an important contribution to the overall picture. Some people are inclined to be very colour conscious. The old saying that a good horse is never a bad colour I'm sure still holds good today. Ideally brown, liver chestnut or a good bay take a lot of beating. A light flashy chestnut will always lose out to a darker colour. Obviously if you breed an animal you will have to put up with its colour, but when going out to buy one opt for the darker colours. Greys are often thought to take a lot of looking after but no more so than do dark horses, which may need extra grooming. Anyway, a grey can always be washed. Obviously in ponies one is going to find more variety than in horses.

Markings can make an animal more appealing, particularly white stars or stripes on the head. White areas on the legs, however, can have an adverse affect.

CONFORMATION

Whatever the size of the animal it needs a quality he
set-on neck which goes well into the shoulder. The e
and bold-looking; nothing looks worse in a horse than

Of all the points needed in a show animal a good n⸺
most important. It should form a natural arch from the wither⸺
poll, being in proportion to the size of the animal. If this arch is inversed,
resulting in what is referred to as an upsidedown or ewe neck, no amount
of schooling or strapping will correct it. If the conformation of the neck
is correct it will be seen even if the horse is in poor condition. A short,
thick neck is to be avoided, because sooner or later the horse will develop
respiratory problems. A long, straight neck is equally undesirable.

Mr Ian Thomas's Lucky Strike II, champion hunter brood mare and winner of no less
than eighty-four championships in her illustrious career. She has outstanding conformation and a particularly good foreleg. Besides her own successes she has bred many
winners, among them a Champion Small Hunter at the Royal International Horse Show.

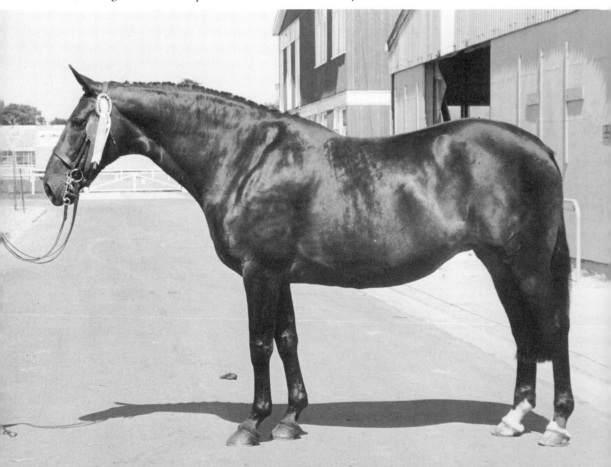

Nearly everyone with any horse knowledge at all knows that a top-class show animal of any type must have a good sloping shoulder with a pronounced wither. Flat withers with loaded shoulders tend to produce a jarring ride and animals with these attributes are often unsound when worked on hard ground. Horses with straight upright shoulders do not stand much work as they are invariably tied and stilty movers. When considering an animal for its quality the one with a bad front and upright loaded shoulders is usually common and plain. The ability to judge a really good shoulder comes from having much experience in hunters and ponies. Many a good showman can camouflage a shoulder in the way he places his saddle and in how his animal is presented to the judge in hand. A very good sloping shoulder usually gives a super ride while a straight shoulder inevitably produces the opposite.

Another example of good all-round conformation: Mr Hugh McCusker's Royal Harvest, a five-year-old, Irish-bred 16.2 hh middleweight show working hunter. This picture was taken after a day's hunting with the Ledbury foxhounds. Later in that same season Royal Harvest became Champion Working Hunter at the South of England Show and won the prestigious Champion Working Hunter title at the Royal Dublin Show. He was subsequently sold to Switzerland as a show jumper. Note also his correct hunter clip.

The back should be short and strong with level quarters and the tail well set on. There should be plenty of room from the hip bone to the croup. The body must have a very good top line with a very slight curve in the spine behind the withers to afford a good comfortable ride. The back should not be hollow or dipped. A roached back, which is the opposite to a hollow back, is also a very bad fault. The ribs should be well sprung, the girth deep and the chest wide. The old grooms used to say that you should be able to fit a broom-head between a horse's front legs (an indication of plenty of heart room). The chest should not be too 'bosomy' for, as Lord Daresbury once said, 'Bosoms are found on tarts not horses.' An animal with a narrow chest, a short girth or a belly that runs up to the hind legs should be avoided at all costs. The loins should be strong and sound with no lightness behind the saddle. The quarters should be well developed and the second thighs strong, well-muscled up and carrying plenty of flesh. An animal short of second thigh looks weak behind.

Forelegs which are 'back at the knee' are a major fault in the show animal. It is an incorrectness which gives the impression of the leg being concave from the knee to the fetlock when viewed from the side. It is also known as calf knees. All leg joints should be clean, free from any puffiness or signs of faulty bone formation. It is on the pastern bones that high and low ringbone occur, something which must not be present in the show animal. Pasterns should be short and slightly sloping to give a more comfortable ride. Upright pasterns, both in front and behind, do not wear well and should be avoided. The size of bone below the knee will determine the amount of weight which the horse is built to carry and will be the limiting factor when choosing a weight-carrying show horse. Good, short cannon bones are favoured.

The knees should be flat and pronounced, not round and small. Joints and surrounding tendons should be firm to the touch and flat with no swelling or roundness whatsoever.

The horse's hind legs, which are his 'engine', should follow a vertical line from the top of the tail to the point of the hocks through the back of the pasterns to the ground. Any type of curb is a sign of weakness as well as being an unsoundness and therefore unacceptable if found on an intended exhibit. Never be tempted to buy a horse if he has (or his conformation predisposes) any sign of a curb. A splint, on the other hand, is a blemish rather than an unsoundness. Weak or badly formed hocks can lead to bog spavins, soft fillings on the front of the joint, or to bone spavins, found on the inside of the hock. Thoroughpins are also found on weak hock joints in the form of soft swellings just in front of the point of the hock. They are sometimes referred to as 'throughpins' because they can be pushed from one side of the hock to the other.

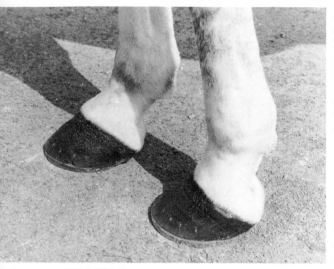

left   Short upright pasterns, normally associated with common animals. Note also the low, weak heel and long toe of the foot. A good blacksmith may well help the latter problems with correct foot dressing.

below left   This horse's forelegs are back at the knee – a common fault which is well-defined here.

below centre   A long, sloping pastern. This type of pastern usually gives a smooth, comfortable ride but can soon show a lot of wear.

below right   Upright forelegs showing a splint on the near fore and small boxy feet, all of which can lead to unsoundness.

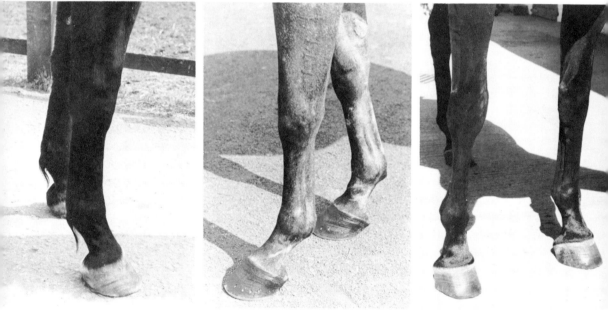

The more common faults in the hock joint are sickle and cow hocks. The former is when the leg below the hock goes in front of the vertical in such a way as to place it further underneath the animal, creating a weakness of that limb. Cow hocks are those which turn inwards as a result of the hind feet pointing outwards. These are better identified from behind the horse. Hocks which from a lateral aspect stand behind the aforementioned vertical line, should also be avoided because they rarely correct themselves even in the young horse.

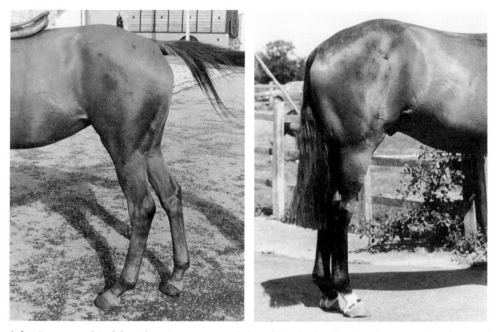

left Incorrect hind leg showing too much bend in the hock. This horse is also short of second thigh and has weak hindquarters. *right* This horse has a good straight hind leg with clean pasterns. It is noticeable that this horse's foot is in need of the farrier. The hindquarters, however, are rather sloping and the tail low set.

Finally we come to the feet – although, strictly speaking, when examining a horse for correctness you should always start here. The old saying 'No foot, no horse' is still very true today. The show animal should have nice round feet, neither too large nor too small for the size of horse. Small, upright, 'boxy' feet are not favoured in the show ring.

Of all the conformational faults found in the horse among the most common are low sloping quarters, often with a jumping bump; long plain heads; too much length in the back; and, of course, curbs. Bad action, also frequently met, has no place in the show ring. Animals who turn their toes in are more acceptable as they are not likely to knock themselves, whereas those who turn them out and stand at 'ten to two' are inclined to strike into themselves, perhaps even falling down in the process. Grooms in the past used to say that a horse with pintoes and a woman who turns her toes out usually made good workers! Of the more critical faults narrow chests, seen on shallow, herring-gutted creatures, are one of the worst as such horses often have weak constitutions as well. A horse with flat sides is invariably more difficult to maintain in good condition than one with a round rib cage.

2

Height Measurement

It is of the utmost importance that show animals in restricted-height classes are measured correctly.

Rules

The rules as laid down by the Joint Measurement Scheme state that:

The animal must have all four shoes removed and the feet must be correctly prepared and balanced as for shoeing.

The owner should as far as possible ensure that the area where the measurement is to take place will be free from avoidable disturbances and distractions which might unsettle the animal.

The animal should be presented for measurement in a headcollar without a bit.

The animal should be handled quietly and allowed to relax before measurement is attempted.

The animal should be positioned for measurement with the front legs parallel and perpendicular; the toes of the front feet should be in line, allowing not more than 1.5 cm (3 in.) above the highest point of the withers.

The measurement must be taken at the highest point of the withers.

Successful Measuring

It is pointless asking an appointed veterinary surgeon to come to your premises to measure your horse or pony for its official certificate until you have done your groundwork. This means having accustomed your animal to being approached by a strange person with a measuring stick and standing still while it is placed on the withers. Practise this several times a day with a young and nervous animal to get him used to it. Failure to do this can make half an inch difference to his height – he could give a false reading if upset. Hair also needs to be taken off the point of the withers.

Many people become worried and land themselves in grave difficulties with the authorities for various reasons when trying to re-measure. Often

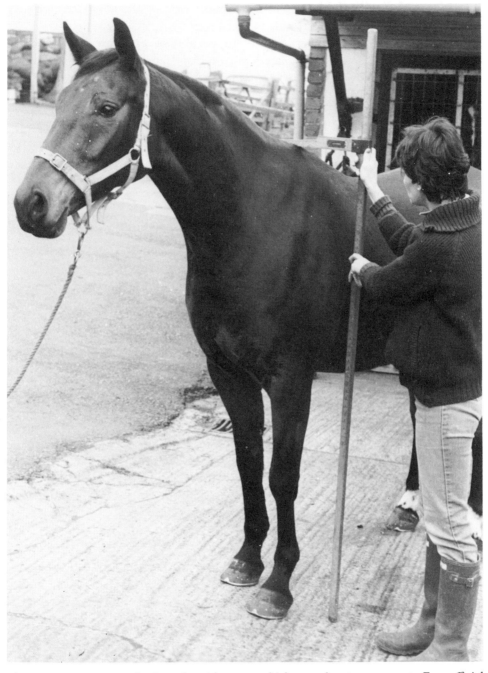

The correct point on the horse's withers at which to take measurement. For official measurement all four shoes should be removed, the horse's head must be in line with its withers and the measuring to be carried out on a level piece of ground.

an animal can measure as much as an inch higher when excited or in a strange place. The same animal, relaxed and carefully prepared, will be the correct height. If it happens to be your first attempt at measuring officially, approach an experienced person for help. You are unlikely to be turned down if your request is made in a business-like manner.

As you will appreciate, a pony that is an eighth of an inch over height very rarely stands any chance in the next division of height, even if the regulations allow him to compete. In the case of 14.2 hh ponies, this would rule them out of pony classes altogether and could, of course, make many thousands of pounds' difference to their value. The same can happen in all classes of horses requiring an official certificate. When purchasing horses with restricted heights for the show ring, remember that, if they are under six years old, there is always a chance of their maturing and being unable to make the height for next season. Much depends on the way the animals have been fed previously, and if you are aware of them always having been done well they are less likely to go over height. A horse that has been on poor pasture and is then fed on corn and good grass is likely to grow rapidly.

I, along with many other people, feel outraged when an exhibit, often for reasons unknown, gets objected to in the middle of the season, for it is at this time that the animal will be at its best, both mentally and physically, and if it has plenty of presence it often appears higher than it actually measures. On the other hand, I have no patience with the odd few people who endeavour to show animals that somehow or another manage to get under the required height. We have all heard about how, in the old days, good or bad people taught their horses by methods fair or foul to go lower when a measuring stick was put on their withers. One cruel method supposedly used by unscrupulous people was to leave weights on the withers in the hope that their poor unfortunate animals would shrink. Today, of course, we hope that these cruel tricks have left us for good. By and large, exhibitors and breeders alike now accept the fact when one of their animals is over its official height and will usually try to place it in a suitable home.

OFFICIAL OBJECTIONS

An objection against a joint measurement certificate under certain rules may only be lodged at a show by an adult exhibitor who has an animal competing in the class in question, or by the chairman or secretary on behalf of the show executive. In addition an objection may be lodged by the judges of the class in question through the secretary of the show. In the absence of the exhibitor or in the event of the exhibitor being a minor, the objection may be made by a representative. When an objection is laid at a show against an animal holding a life certificate, the following procedure must be carried out by the objector: a deposit of £75 must be sent to the secretary of the Joint Measurement Scheme by first-class mail and posted within twenty-four hours. The secretary will initiate the re-measurement procedure on receipt of the deposit. If the objection is upheld, the deposit will be returned to the objector.

Arranging a Re-measurement

The secretary of the Joint Measurement Scheme will arrange for the re-measurement to take place at the earliest possible date. The senior referee will arrange an appointment for this with the owner and will notify the secretary of the Joint Measurement Scheme. The secretary will inform the Joint Measurement Scheme steward, who will attend, of the time and place of the re-measurement, and also, if applicable, the objector.

When a life certificate is issued for an animal that has been re-measured by referees for whatever reason, that animal cannot be re-measured again under the rules of the Joint Measurement Scheme. When an annual certificate is issued for an animal that has been re-measured by referees for whatever reason, that animal cannot be re-measured again in the same year.

If you are showing youngstock, they have to be measured on the showground and you are completely in the hands of the vet of the day. Young animals can vary in height from show to show for many different reasons if they are right up to height, as many of the top animals are. These measurements have to be taken literally on the day of showing in the case of youngsters, because at leading shows no official certificate is allowed. This, of course, is one of the interesting aspects of showing – one has to face the ups and downs, sometimes literally!

One thing that upsets the showing world is when an animal is offered for sale at a certain height but after it has changed hands it is recorded in print as higher or lower. This does seem to set the cat among the pigeons and can start a lot of unpleasantness. However, much depends on where and when an animal was measured and by whom. The conformation of a horse or pony can even be responsible for making it visibly higher or lower as quite a few have high or low withers, but just as many, particularly cobs and certain ponies, have flat withers. At a small show there can be animals very much under the required height, so that one well-produced horse or pony up to the full height can, to the outside, look very large and consequently get quite unnecessarily objected to.

3
Health and Welfare

Before dealing with specific areas for care and attention in the show animal I want to start this chapter by pointing out the main reasons why so many horses have short-lived careers in the show ring. Those who follow the show circuit will know that whilst a few animals go on for year after year, many more come out for a season and then are not heard of again. There are, of course, many explanations for this but the chief causes are the animal's temperament and hard ground. A factor which is often overlooked is that a horse with a hot and difficult temperament will require a considerable amount of work before it can enter the ring in a settled frame of mind. If this work is carried out during the summer when the ground is hard, damage to joints and feet can occur. If the animal suffers any 'jarring' in his limbs he will tend to shorten his stride and feel very sore when ridden by the judge. This is frequently seen in the ring when the going is like concrete. Hard ground also makes some animals go with their ears back, looking sour and obviously hating every moment of it. Whilst some older animals do not appear to mind working on hard going it is especially important to take great care where younger animals are concerned.

I personally think it is criminal to see youngstock being lunged in small, tight circles on rock-hard ground at shows. I am convinced that some people think this is the right thing to do because they have seen others doing it. In other cases, the extra lungeing is carried out because the animal is overfresh, overfed and has never been taught manners at home. If a horse does not do as he is told at home, no way will he behave in public. Firm handling from the start, and, if required, one good stripe with a cane, is all that should be necessary to make the animal not only behave but also respect you.

Hints on riding-in before a class are given on page 105.

TEETH

In my own yard I insist that great care is paid to my animals' teeth. I have a professional horse dentist or veterinary surgeon examine the horses' mouths twice a year and I leave it to the experts as to what should be done. Sharp edges on teeth can make an animal one-sided or fussy in its mouth; or it may have wolf teeth that need to be removed. These small teeth are easily dealt with and can make all the difference to a horse's way of going. From my own experience any soreness in the mouth can be very painful, and I believe this is true with horses. Until the animal is rested and all soreness gone it is pointless to continue riding that horse for I am convinced that to do so leads to head shaking and other troubles.

If an animal is not eating the quantity of hay you think it should, or if it throws its feed about and seems to spit it out (often called 'quidding'), the horse's teeth may be to blame. Sharp edges on the molar teeth can be the cause of horses not putting on condition and feeding badly. This problem particularly affects older animals. Also, it is quite possible for an older horse or pony to develop a decayed tooth, and you can imagine the pain it has to suffer if this continues unnoticed and unattended. So, obviously, the need for very careful and regular attention to teeth is vital to a happy contented show horse.

WORMS

These days worming seems to be more important than ever possibly because people are now better informed about the dangers of worm damage. Nevertheless, one still hears of horses and ponies dying as a result of worm damage and of the many bouts of colic and scouring in the spring which the vet has to deal with.

Much of the trouble is caused by red worm, which are passed in the dung in vast quantity. The speed at which the worm eggs develop into larvae depends on the temperature and humidity. Over the winter little development occurs but in the spring activity begins and this is the time when animals become reinfested and are at their most vulnerable. The adult worms attach themselves to the gut wall and suck blood. Heavy worm infestation causes such loss of blood that anaemia develops. The constant battle to replace that blood causes the animal to lose weight rapidly even though it is receiving a lot to eat. Often the eyes look very dull and the coat becomes dry, staring and lifeless. Sometimes small ulcers develop in the intestines and this in turn leads to scouring, which can become so chronic that the animal becomes severely distressed.

Because you cannot see worms in a horse's droppings it does not mean the animal is worm-free. If worm eggs are detected in the dung then mature worms and larvae must be present to produce them. If I am in any doubt about the presence of worms I normally have my vet take a blood test and take his advice as to treatment. Sometimes it is necessary to administer large doses of wormer to clear up an infestation and free the unfortunate host from this awful menace.

Whatever brand of wormer you choose you must worm your horse regularly and follow the maker's recommendations. Whether the form you use is a powder, paste or granules it won't alter the wormer's effectiveness but the convenience with which it is given. Some animals have only to sniff worm powder to put them off their feed altogether, so in this case paste in a modern syringe would be easier to administer – and of course you would know that the animal had received it.

After worming it is a good idea to keep your animal in for a few days to help keep paddocks as worm-free as possible. If you are lucky enough to have fresh paddocks that have not had horses on them for some time, this will help keep the worm problem at bay. Nevertheless the worming routine should never be overlooked. Picking up dung from pastures is a tedious job but it is invaluable not only in freeing them from worms but also in keeping them sweet.

As horses and ponies become older they do build up a partial, natural immunity.

When loosing out show horses care must be taken they do not career about and injure themselves.

Turning Out

With stabled show animals it is essential to loose them out for a period of time each day, depending on weather conditions etc. Obviously on a wet, windy day there is no point turning out clipped ridden horses, but youngstock do better if they go out daily and certainly look forward to their period of freedom. If youngsters have to stay in for any length of time they can become so fresh that when loosed they gallop and fool about and it is then that accidents happen. When only one youngster is to go out (and in the case of a hunter) it will benefit from the company of a quiet pony. Providing your horse has a reasonably safe, well-fenced field in which to be turned out, no harm should come to him.

When a show animal full of the joys of spring is let out usually it will buck and kick, have a roll and a gallop. This is so good for horses, mentally and physically, that it is precisely why we go to the trouble of turning them out. If you do not – and I'm afraid there are some people who think their animals are too valuable to let out in the summer – they will only get more and more fresh. As a result you will have to work them more, so making them fitter, and in the end you have created a vicious circle.

One way of safeguarding against injury caused when galloping loose is to turn a horse out with docile company.

It is most important with a show animal to keep it happy and quiet. Between shows ridden animals can have several days off from riding altogether in order to unwind after a show, especially if they have had to travel long distances and have been away from home for a few days. These considerations are part and parcel of caring for the show horse and are essential if you want a happy, well-conditioned, contented creature who is a pleasure to own. Some show animals are a positive liability not only to their owners but to others around them. We have all seen at shows, exhibitors with animals they cannot and will not control, screaming 'Keep away from my horse!', when in fact they and their ill-mannered animals are the ones who should stay away from the show.

Safe, well-built fencing is a priority for the welfare of horses and ponies.

Often in the heat of the summer when flies are worrying horses and ponies, it is preferable to turn animals out at night and bring them in during the daytime. Youngstock and mares and foals benefit enormously from this routine and can even go out the night before and after a show. However, be careful not to turn them out late if they have been travelling as they might well be on the hot side and could easily catch a chill.

Many people successfully show horses and ponies from the field, especially youngstock, bringing them in the night before a show. Any extra feeding can be done in the field if this best suits your needs. It is of course the natural place for them to be and many champions have been so produced. I must admit that I prefer this method, especially for horses who are destined for some other competitive sphere later in life. Horses who are cosseted like hot-house plants can grow up to be soft and gutless, thus rendering them useless outside the show ring and unable to do a job of work.

Although stock-proof this type of fencing is not recommended for horses and ponies because of the risk of injury on the wire.

Coughs and Respiratory Problems

If ever you have any doubts about an animal's health, in particular if it goes off its feed, looks sick or sorry or starts to cough, it is wise to call your vet immediately. A delay can not only make matters worse but also postpone the horse's return to work and shows. On no account should an animal be taken to a show if there are uncertainties as to either soundness or illness. To travel an animal which is not one hundred per cent right can lead to it being taken very ill. If it should have a temperature, a journey can cause untold troubles later. In addition you run the risk of infecting any animals with which it is travelling, and others at the show as well. To ride a horse or pony that shows signs of lifelessness or coughs more than once or twice could result in permanent heart and lung troubles. Larger horses are particularly susceptible to wind damage and can easily be left with a chronic cough. A horse or pony that makes a noise in its wind or is in any way wrong in its wind is rendered useless in the show ring. Moreover any kind of wind operation will mean that a horse or pony is ineligible for affiliated society shows. In the show ring there is often controversy as to whether an animal makes a noise or not. Some do when they get excited, especially if they overbend and tuck their noses into their chests, but the same horses when relaxed and going quietly may be perfectly noise-free. Before or after a horse has had a virus or if it has suffered a long bout of coughing and is brought into work too soon is another time when a slight noise may be heard. This is where an owner, particularly if he or she is inexperienced, can get into real trouble.

The larger the horse the more care one has to take with his wind. This is why many heavyweight show horses disappear from the ring after a season or two. It is a great art to keep them right while in show condition, able to withstand the constant galloping that is required of them. If a horse or pony starts coughing, besides taking veterinary advice it is essential to dampen all feeds, especially the hay. It may also be beneficial to bed the horse on shavings as this reduces dust levels in the stable and prevents the animal from picking at his straw bed which in turn could irritate the cough. The treatment of sick horses should be on the same lines as for humans. It is no good seeking advice and then not taking it.

There is obviously a difference between a noise which is caused by an animal being thick in its wind through lack of work or through carrying too much fat, and one which is a genuine defect. It is only by experience that one can tell, so if in doubt seek expert advice.

LAMENESS AND LEG PROBLEMS

Many horses and ponies are annually sent out of the ring by judges because of lameness. In addition ringside critics are frequently heard proclaiming that such and such a horse was lame at a recent certain somewhere. Some obviously are lame, either temporarily or permanently, and the causes can be manifold: it could be from a knock; or from treading on a sharp stone, or from picking up an old nail on the show ground (it has happened more than once); a sprain; or from an unsoundness whose cause is unknown.

At evening stables always make a point of running your hand down each leg to check for any sign of heat or filling. Heat in a leg is an indication of trouble, so if you find it don't be surprised if next morning your animal pulls out lame. Lameness is often very difficult to detect even for those with vast experience, and discovering whether in fact the horse is lame in front or behind can be no easy matter. If lameness is acute it is far easier to diagnose but with a slightly lame animal it may only be seen when the horse is on the turn.

Horses do not place their weight on the leg which is causing them pain. If there is no heat or filling in the leg, the foot must then be suspect. Firstly, it is wise to call your vet or farrier to remove the shoe. The cause could be a nail bind or prick, especially if the horse is freshly shod. For this reason it is prudent, particularly for an important show, to have your horse shod several days beforehand, then at least you should not arrive at a show with a lame exhibit. It may also be that the shoe has been fitted too tightly or is pressing on the sole of a sensitive animal. In larger animals in particular, corns in the heels will often cause lameness; and frequently the cause of corns is from owners leaving shoes on too long and allowing the heel of the shoe to sink into the foot.

If a horse happens to be lame in the foot for the above reasons or from a bruise, there is nothing better than to stand the foot in a bucket of warm water with a handful of common salt for ten to thirty minutes. A bran poultice can also be applied with the help of an old sack, or better still, if you own or can borrow one, a poultice boot which is made for the job. This can be left on all night and taken off in the morning, and the foot then soaked in water for about thirty minutes. If necessary you can poultice the foot, day and night, for three days (after which apply at night only). Should there be no improvement when the horse is trotted up, it could mean it has either a poisoned foot or the trouble is more serious. If so, you will, of course, have to be guided by your vet.

It may well be that if the problem is not in the foot your animal is putting up a splint. This applies particularly to young ridden animals. It is often when putting one up that they go lame and at this stage the splint is difficult to detect. If you run your thumb down the cannon bone and the animal flinches when you find a sore spot, a splint could be to blame. Rest will be essential to avoid long-term damage, otherwise the lameness will persist and eventually the horse will throw a larger and more unsightly splint. Hunters can usually be forgiven an old small splint but hacks and pony judges do not like them at all. Remember, a splint is only a blemish; it is not an unsoundness if the animal is not lame.

Unfortunately many show animals, particularly when they get older, suffer from more serious foot and leg problems. One of the worst is navicular, a disease of the foot for which, in my opinion, there is no cure. Careful shoeing and restricted work on soft ground may lengthen the period of use but usually once navicular has been diagnosed it is very difficult to show the unfortunate animal again – and, of course, Bute is not allowed in the show ring. A horse with navicular is best doing a quiet hacking job as the hard ground and the need to work for the show ring offers little hope. Navicular is usually confined to the fore feet. Animals who come out of the stable lame or 'footy' but who loosen up with work are navicular suspects. Having the feet X-rayed by an experienced vet is the quickest and kindest way of diagnosing this disease.

Warfarin has been used throughout the world as a treatment for navicular and an estimated fifty per cent of sufferers have, for a time, returned to work. Horses receiving Warfarin need to have their blood-clotting rates checked every six weeks because Warfarin thins the blood. This treatment requires dedication and great experience on the owner's part. If the horse is insured against permanent loss of use some insurance companies will insist that this treatment is tried before any claims are accepted. I have tried using Warfarin on two show hunters of mine but both were unsuccessfully treated.

Sprained tendons and ligaments are other causes of lameness. Both will create heat and great pain in the affected limb and are often caused by impact on hard ground, a severe jar or a wrench. Animals which have a tendency to roll in their boxes often become lame, a result of getting cast. Whatever the cause rest the animal at once – failure to do so could easily cause further damage – and endeavour to reduce the inflammation by alternating hot poultices with cold-water douches and cold-water bandages. It is useful to place gamgee tissue under the bandages as this will retain more water and help to cool the legs. Cold hosing is also very beneficial.

It is advisable to seek veterinary advice for any suspected sprain. To put an animal back into work too quickly could cause lasting damage. The sprain may well be deep-seated but it would be difficult for the amateur to know this. If sufficient care is not taken, a valuable show animal could end up with a bowed tendon which would render it useless in the show ring.

Lameness caused by laminitis is dealt with on page 40.

Nothing looks more unsightly than a hock which has been in any way capped. It is not an unsoundness but it looks awful and is very difficult to get rid of. It consists of a soft swelling over the point of the hock and can vary from being almost undetectable to the size of the proverbial football. It is due to an increase in the fluid content of the subcutaneous bursa (synovial sac) under the tendon. Occasionally it is due to thickening of the tendon sheath, in which case it is readily distinguished by its hardness.

Because of the prominent position of the hock it is particularly prone to injury from knocks, from kicking in the stable or from lying down on insufficient bedding. Generally the injury is self-inflicted. Once a swelling on the hock becomes sizeable it is one of the most difficult blemishes to reduce. Lameness seldom occurs even with very large swellings. In treating animals for capped hocks, if recently done, hot and cold applications will help enormously, followed by astringent lotions. Massage with a proprietary reducer will help lessen the swelling. Veterinary advice should also be sought as in some cases it may be possible to drain away some of the fluid and replace it with cortisone.

INJURIES

If for any reason your show horse or pony sustains a knock or cut of any kind, no effort should be spared in nursing the animal back to health. Often an injury may appear quite trivial at first but if it should leave a blemish there will be times when this will go against the horse. Some judges obviously place more store than others on the site of an injury, i.e. if it is in a vulnerable place such as a joint, knee or hock.

Extra care must be taken after accidents etc. to allow the animal time to recover to full fitness. To show or work the horse too soon is to risk putting it out of action for a considerable time. Moreover it could be damaging to the horse's future because if a judge puts the animal out or down the line the whole showground is a-buzz (this particularly applies to champion animals) and before you know it the animal is condemned for the rest of the season. It is, therefore, far better to miss one or two shows and err on the side of caution.

Always seek expert advice at the time of an injury. To delay treatment of the right kind will, in the long run, be more expensive in terms of shows missed and winning form etc.

First aid is dealt with on page 99.

4

Stable Management

The Stable

From the moment a horse or pony comes into a stable, permanently or temporarily, every care should be taken for his well-being and comfort. The actual position of the building is often a matter of necessity rather than choice. Aim for well-ventilated (but not draughty) stables, if possible facing south. Most horse owners have to put up with whatever accommodation is available for their animals, but they can make improvements to ventilation and prevent damp. Ideally the size of the box should be 10ft × 10ft for ponies and 12ft × 12ft for horses. Large 17 hh heavyweights will need a box 14ft × 14ft.

There are many different makes and designs of stable building on the market now and all have their different uses for various types of horses and ponies. Prices start from around £300 for a portable, wooden box. Concrete blocks can make excellent boxes if well designed and built, though the ultimate in luxury is bricks and mortar.

It is advisable to fit iron vees or mesh grilles to the top of your stable doors. One reason is to prevent chewing of the doors or side pieces as this can lead to crib-biting or wind-sucking, particularly in youngstock. Both are very bad stable vices which are easily passed from one horse to another, considerably lowering the animals' value. Weaving is another stable vice which can be learnt as a result of having no top grille in the doors. These and other bad habits are caught or learnt through boredom – show horses in top condition spend a lot of their time indoors and easily get bored. Remember: prevention is better than cure.

Where schooling facilities are concerned, it is convenient to have access to an indoor or outdoor school, though by no means essential. In fact, all schooling can be done in a good-sized paddock. Remember that many champion horses and ponies have been and always will be produced from very limited facilities. The main thing is to have a good surface on which to school, one that does not get rock-hard, particularly in summer.

Hay Racks versus Nets

Always opt for a hay rack fitted in the corner of your box in preference to using a hay net. There is a danger of horses, particularly youngstock, getting a leg caught up in·a net with disastrous results – perhaps when they are rolling or if they paw the ground when eating and if the net has not been tied high enough. A new tarred net, well tied and hung, will not easily give way. In fact, it is the best policy to give all youngstock their hay loose on the floor, which is both natural and prevents any tendency to develop unwanted muscle on the neck.

MANGERS

Should a manger be sited on the stable floor or in the corner at a height to suit the individual horse? The system of feeding at floor level is becoming more and more popular because it seems the most natural. Whichever position you opt for, it is most important that the manger is large enough to prevent feed being thrown out and then eaten off the floor later after it has become soiled.

Mangers should always be kept clean: horses have an acute sense of smell and dirty mangers can harbour musty relics of past feeds, which could be very off-putting. You should never put fresh feeds on top of old half-eaten ones either.

BEDDING

There are two main materials used today in stables for bedding: straw and wood shavings. Straw, without doubt, if first-class and long, is ideal in that not only is it quite easily managed, making an excellent bed, but it looks good too. Horses always appear happy in it. Straw has the added advantage that it is more easily disposed of. It is of great use as a fertiliser, whereas shavings are practically impossible to get rid of and nobody wants to take them away. In time one has either to pay someone to remove soiled shavings or find a use for them oneself.

When using straw, make sure the bed is deep enough to safeguard against capped hocks. It is false economy to save money on bedding. Care must be taken when mucking out to take only soiled straw and replace with fresh so that the horse has at all times a deep bed with plenty round the sides. Wheat straw is best, although some people now use barley; oat straw should never be used as it can cause colic and skin irritation. The only real drawback of straw bedding is that some horses tend to pick at or even eat it, and ponies are apt to gorge it if on a restricted diet: this is not a problem if you use shavings. Remember that horses are more likely to eat new season's straw than old.

In the last few years wood shavings have grown in popularity as bedding material. The advantages are that they can easily be purchased in polythene sacks from many sources, in quantities varying from one bale to a five-hundred-bale load. Obviously the more that can be purchased at one time, the cheaper the price, which can be from £2 to £4 per bale. Wood shavings can be stored outside and do not have to be kept under cover. Unlike straw, their quality is consistently good.

In my own yard I keep half my horses on wheat straw, which is purchased off local farms in the autumn, and the other half on shavings. I find this the best system because I can vary the bedding to suit the needs of different horses. Straw seems better suited to youngstock as they spend more time out of their boxes and tend to dig at their beds, making quite a mess if they are on shavings.

When using wood shavings, you must start with a good, deep bed. If you begin with too little, your horses will be lying on the bare floor by the time they have walked and kicked the bedding about. An average-sized box will need approximately six bales to get the required depth. It is advisable to dampen the shavings with a hose in the summer to prevent dust and help to keep them in place.

Having started your bed, you have to decide if you are prepared to keep it spotless, picking up every dropping and taking away wet patches. If you wish, you can also turn over the bed, which always looks neat and clean but is very time-consuming. My own method is to pick up all droppings several times a day and add clean shavings when necessary, so creating a sort of semi-deep litter. With a clean and tidy horse, this can work very well. Some of my boxes are mucked out only once a year, while others have just the middles taken out once a month. By trial and error you will find out what suits you best. Once a shavings bed is established it is very easy to manage with a reasonably clean and coop-erative horse. On the other hand, if the horse is very dirty and digs at its bed, it is best to put it on straw.

STABLE-YARD TOOLS

To avoid inconvenience and arguments the stable should have its own tools which should not be shared with the house or the farm. They should all be of good quality.

First you will require a large shovel and, if using both straw and shavings as bedding, a three-pronged fork. If straw only is used, a two-pronged fork is much easier to handle when shaking up beds. You will also need a good yard broom and either a basket or a plastic skip for the droppings. You will probably require a wheelbarrow, which can be of any type to suit your own individual needs. When mucking out straw, some people prefer to carry away the soiled bedding in a muck sheet. The

Yard work at the Oliver stables.

muck heap should, of course, always be neat and well stacked. A good yard is always matched by its tidy muck heap.

WATERING

As regards watering, much depends on the individual horse, his work and his stable routine. A horse cannot have too much water if allowed to have free access to it at all times. It is only when his consumption is restricted that problems can occur and colic might result, for example a horse might drink himself full after travelling long distances without water or after fast work. Many people now give their horses constant access to water via automatic drinking bowls without any adverse effects. There are many good examples on the market and you should have no difficulty in finding a suitable type. These bowls should be checked at least twice a day to ensure that water is flowing and that they are kept scrupulously clean. They are extremely time-saving and have the added advantage that they cannot be tipped over.

If buckets are used for watering, they should be large and as heavy as possible. Secure them, perhaps with a bar, to prevent them being tipped up. Horses should be watered at regular intervals if on buckets and always

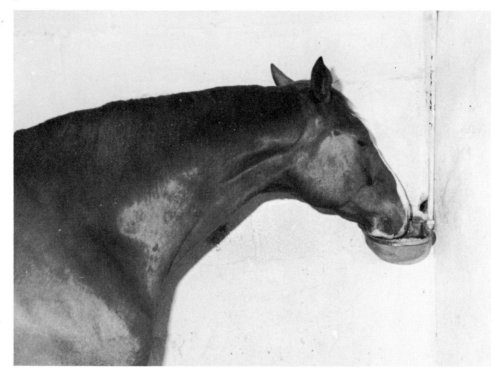

A horse making use of an automatic water bowl.

before feeding. They should be allowed as much as they wish. To water after feeding is bad for digestion and can cause colic. A horse cannot have too much water but certainly can have too little. In good stable management a bucket should always stand full in the corner. There is no harm in giving the horse or pony a bucketful of water after exercise or travelling but ideally he should never work for several hours after drinking a large quantity. Care must be taken to ensure that each horse has its own bucket otherwise coughs, colds and other ailments can spread very easily; under no circumstances should a horse or pony use or drink from a bucket that is likely to carry infection. The obvious advantage of buckets is that they enable you to gauge how much your horse is (or is not) drinking, and if you need to add any medicine to his water it can easily be done.

To sum up, water and watering is one of the most important factors in good stable management. A horse will survive without food for some considerable time, but will quickly deteriorate if he is short of water.

5
Feeding

The main items of feed for the show animal are discussed below, but it is up to the individual to find out by trial and error what suits his or her animals best. The saying 'One man's meat is another man's poison' still holds true: whereas a hunter will require plenty of bulk and concentrates, a hack or pony will need far less in comparison. Feeding is an art which cannot be learnt overnight.

HAY

After water (already discussed in the stable management chapter – page 37), hay is the next priority, depending on the type of horse or pony and what work he has to do. You have to gauge whether he requires top-class seed (essential for show hunters), hard hay, or can make do, as most ponies can, with soft meadow hay. Whichever type, it must be well made and dust free, and should be fed at the right time of year – that is, new season's hay should not be fed before 1st December of the year of making. If it is, you run the risk of filled legs, stomach disorders and scouring. Good hay should always smell nice and sweet and feel good to handle. Poor, musty-looking hay lacking in aroma is a worthless feed and on no account should ever be given to stabled horses.

The purchasing of hay in small quantities is not always an easy matter unless you have access to a merchant or a good friendly farmer. Choose your merchant with care; if you buy regularly from one supplier he is more likely to try to maintain a regular supply of good-quality feed.

It is of no use whatsoever buying expensive cereal feeds and feeding additives at random if you are not prepared to buy and feed the best hay, which in the long run is always the cheapest. Experience will soon teach you to identify top-quality hay and feedstuffs, as will your horse if he empties his rack and licks his manger clean. Haylage is a relatively new alternative to conventional hay and, although it is comparatively more expensive, it is particularly beneficial for horses with a respiratory problem.

Ad lib hay for stabled show horses relieves boredom and lessens any tendency towards stable vices.

Oats

In the feeding of hunters and hunter youngstock it is difficult to better rolled oats which, besides being a traditional horse feed, are so much more suitable than other grains in their proportion of starch, protein and fibre. The digestibility of oats is improved by rolling them or even crushing them, which causes the animal to eat them more slowly. If his oats are unrolled, a horse will probably bolt them and a certain amount will pass through him undigested, as will be seen from his droppings.

Feeding oats to show hunters helps to keep them in hard condition to withstand the galloping they are required to do. Obviously if your hunter is sharp and gassy in the ring and tends to hot up, he will require no oats or only small amounts. The quantity which should be fed to show hunters varies considerably with their size and temperament. Remember that whole oats can be boiled in the same way as barley, which takes the heating effect out of them and makes them into really good-value feed.

Barley

As a fattening feed, barley without doubt has no equal. Rolled barley can be fed but in very small amounts of 1–2lb as it is heating to a horse's system and will cause him to rub and feel uncomfortable if given in large quantities, particularly in the spring and summer. Cooked barley, on the other hand, is a wonderful conditioner, easily digestible and, when mixed with a bran mash, makes a very palatable feed indeed, readily eaten by horses and ponies alike.

It is now possible to buy cooked flaked barley – or, as some call it, micronised barley – from your corn merchant. This, of course, has the advantage of being ready to use, saving preparation time and trouble. It has been shown to be very successful in getting and keeping condition on show animals.

Great care should be taken in feeding barley and oats to ponies, because if they are not given enough work they can develop laminitis or, as some people call it, fever of the feet, which causes a chronic lameness and is often fatal if not treated immediately by a vet. The first signs of this are when an animal comes out of its stable either lame or going very short in its action. The feet will become very hot and the animal will feel very uncomfortable in general.

Bran

Bran is one of the most important feeds in show stables, but unfortunately it is no longer of the quality that it used to be. The truth is that modern milling takes away much of the goodness that used to be left in the wheat. Nonetheless it still is a useful feed, especially in that it can be made into a bran mash which can be given once or twice a week with Epsom salts added to keep your show animal 'right' inside.

To make a bran mash you will need:

> 3–4lb bran
> 1oz common salt
> handful of Epsom salts

Add 3 pints of boiling water, stir well (should be a crumbly consistency), cover and allow the mixture to stand for 30 minutes or until cooled to blood heat. If by any chance a horse won't eat the salts in a feed, a handful can be added to a bucket of water, but not to an automatic watering bowl.

If you are feeding in the traditional manner with oats, bran and some cooked barley, your horse can have 1–5lb per day of bran, depending on his size.

When buying bran, choose the broad variety, not fine or what is often termed 'pig bran'. It must be stored in a dry place, otherwise it will soon go off and smell musty, which will render it useless. Bran is high in nutriments and minerals, is easy to digest and is a wonderful feed when horses are short of work or laid up for any reason in their stable.

Linseed

Because linseed is very high in fat and oil, it is very good for a horse's coat and digestive system. It is a fattening food as well as a good all-round conditioner. The amount to feed again depends on the size of the animal; it can be up to 2lb per day for a large show hunter. The disadvantage of linseed is in the preparation required – it burns easily and can make an awful mess and an unpleasant smell if it boils over on a stove. There are some makes of boiler stove that can cook barley and linseed together without burning, but these are expensive to buy and run.

In the ordinary way linseed should be soaked for twenty-four hours in cold water prior to cooking for four to five hours until it is jellied. During cooking it should be stirred regularly to prevent it sticking and burning.

I rarely feed linseed nowadays, but it can be useful in exceptional cases where a horse fails to respond well to its diet.

Flaked Maize

Maize is a very heating feed and needs to be fed with great care. If fed in quantity it is known to lead to laminitis, particularly in ponies, and to blood disorders. For these reasons I never use flaked maize in my yard.

Nuts

There are currently many different brands of horse and pony nuts on the market, all with various ingredients and uses. They are marketed in 25kg (55lb) bags, ideal to store and handle, and come with very easy-to-follow instructions as to how much or how little to feed. Nuts provide a balanced diet – indeed, some larger stables, particularly in racing, feed only nuts – but horses and ponies do get bored with them after a time and will not eat the required amount to do themselves justice. You can, however, mix them with a little additive such as soaked beet-pulp and bran to make the feed more interesting.

Sugar-beet Pulp

This is a very good feed additive for show horses, which they relish in the summer when the weather is hot and dry. It contains a lot of goodness and helps keep condition on as well as encouraging horses to eat up their feed. It can be bought in nuts or a shredded form. Sugar-beet pulp must be kept in a safe place where it cannot be reached by a horse or pony while it is dry and unsoaked: if it is eaten in this form, it can cause colic and even death. Before feeding soak for twenty-four hours in sufficient water to moisten well. Care is required in feeding sugar-beet pulp as it can cause the animal's droppings to be very loose: only experience will show how much each animal can take, according to its size, from 1 to 5lb per day.

Never forget that unsoaked sugar beet is a *killer*.

Chaff

As well as aiding digestion, chaff is a useful way of adding bulk to feed, especially for show horses and ponies who tend to bolt while eating and for hacks and small ponies which do not require a lot of hard feed. It is still possible to purchase an old-fashioned hand-turned chaff cutter which is suitable for the small stable, and there are various electric models available for the larger establishment.

New on the market and, it is to be hoped, here to stay is molassed chaff which animals really enjoy in their feed. Being moist and enriched with vitamins, it is a very good additive.

CARROTS

Carrots are an excellent additive to a horse's diet, though rather expensive. Shy and bad feeders are helped by the addition of carrots to their feed. Care should always be taken when feeding these vegetables to horses that they are cut lengthways and not across which can cause choking.

SALT

Horses need salt in their diet, to aid digestion and clear the blood. Ideally, place a lump of old-fashioned rock salt in the horse's manger, or fix a proprietary salt lick somewhere in the horse's loose-box. Alternatively common salt can be added to the daily feed.

GUIDANCE ON FEEDING

The principles of feeding horses and ponies are dealt with in detail in many other handbooks and publications. Here, I will restrict my coverage to the practices adopted in my own yard, giving a few sample diets and some tips.

You must master the art of feeding if you want your show horse to be ready for the ring at the required time. With show animals the aim is to build up the right amount of condition so that they look fit and well covered *but not fat*. Obviously some animals are easier to keep condition on than others. Temperament is an important factor; nervous highly-strung individuals will obviously need more careful feeding than those with placid natures. As stated elsewhere, horses with correct conformation hold their condition and looks better than those who are long backed and narrow.

Modern feed charts are supplied with most manufactured horse feeds but they must be adapted with care and common sense. Try to tailor any suggested diet to suit your individual horse's needs, basing your adjustment on the work he is doing and his energy requirements. Obviously the more hay you give your horse the fewer concentrates he will require. Trial and error will be your guide.

The manner of feeding is almost as important as the feed content: it is no good throwing a bowl or scoop of oats over the stable door and telling the horse to get on with it. Try to adhere to the golden rule of feeding little and often as horses have small stomachs and cannot cope with large, heavy meals. If an animal ever leaves a feed or part of it, remove the remainder and reduce the ration at the next meal. Never, never put new feed on top of old feed as the latter quickly becomes sour and toxic. If eaten by an animal the following day colic and scouring could result. It goes without saying that feed bowls and mangers should be kept scrupulously clean.

If possible you should give three or four feeds per day, depending on your circumstances and the amount of help available in the stable yard. Horses are very adaptable to any time schedule as long as it is regularly kept to as closely as possible. Providing a fourth feed at about 8–9pm is very beneficial as it is the quietest part of the day and the horse can digest his meal in peace. If you do feed at this time give your horse a large feed which he can eat through the night and possibly early morning. Breakfast or the first feed of the day need only be small and made up of a few ingredients which your horse or pony likes best. Follow this at midday with a slightly larger feed, and then at about 5pm give the horse his tea (or his last feed, depending on whether he is fed three or four times a day). In my own yard the horses are fed three times a day with the last meal usually being the largest.

It must be remembered that at the start of the season a horse will feed more easily before he has had to contend with the stress of travelling to shows. In mid-season, when it is very hot, he may also sometimes go off his feed when everything, including grass, has become very dry and dusty.

Given below are the feeding programmes for four different show horses and ponies kept in my yard.

Feed chart for an average, stabled 16.2 hh show hunter (summer)

   ad lib hay

7.30 a.m.   1lb bran
             1½lbs rolled oats
             3lbs horse and pony cubes
             chaff
             ½ scoop soaked sugar-beet pulp

12 noon   ditto

5.00 p.m.   2lb bran
             2lbs rolled oats
             3lbs horse and pony cubes
             chaff
             1 scoop sugar-beet pulp

To the foregoing I might add either 3lbs per day of cooked flaked barley or 3lbs of whole barley cooked on a stove. This would be of benefit to horses who are short of condition.

Feed chart for an average, stabled 13.2 hh pony (summer)

ad lib hay

7.30 a.m.	½lb bran 2lbs horse and pony cubes chaff ½ scoop sugar-beet pulp
12 noon	ditto
5.00 p.m.	1lb bran 2lbs horse and pony cubes chaff ½ scoop sugar-beet pulp

Beware of overfeeding ponies, especially in spring, as it can lead to laminitis.

Feed chart for an average, stabled 15.2 hh hack (summer)

For show hacks I always leave out oats and replace them by rolled or micronised barley.

ad lib hay

7.30 a.m.	1lb bran 1½lbs horse and pony cubes 2lbs rolled barley chaff ½ scoop sugar-beet pulp
12 noon	ditto
5.00 p.m.	1½lbs bran 2lbs horse and pony cubes 3lbs rolled barley chaff 1 scoop sugar-beet pulp

Feed chart of Seabrook, Champion Hunter, Horse of the Year Show 1984

During the show season this 17 hh heavyweight was receiving:

ad lib hay

7.30 a.m.   1½lbs bran
             3lbs horse and pony cubes
             1lb cooked flaked barley
             3lbs oats
             1 scoop molasses
             chaff
             1 scoop sugar-beet pulp

12 noon   ditto

5.00 p.m.   ditto

6

Grooming

A would-be show horse or pony must be well groomed regularly. Depending on the time available, one can spend approximately thirty to sixty minutes a day grooming in order not only to help to improve the circulation and keep the skin healthy but also to maintain the coat in tip-top condition. Always remember, however, that no amount of shampooing or grooming will be of any benefit if your horse is not well fed and 'right' inside.

Before starting to groom, tie the animal up. Begin systematically at the neck and work all over the body, first with a rubber curry comb to loosen the coat and then lightly with a dandy brush. After this you can then start the real work of body brushing which, if done correctly using plenty of elbow grease, will really clean and put a shine on your animal. The length of time put into body brushing is up to the individual. Some horses and ponies are obviously cleaner than others. A lot too depends on the type of coat the animal has. Many people have a sponge or piece of sacking and a bucket of warm water handy and periodically damp the horse all over during body brushing to help remove dirt and grease. This method is especially successful in the summer when horses' coats are fine.

When you have completed the body, go on to the legs and finally the head. The animal can then be strapped or finished off with a stable rubber to remove any dust. Lastly, sponge out the eyes, nose and dock. Pick out the feet and apply a proprietary brand of hoof oil. In show animals, great care must be paid to the tail as careless brushing with a dandy will result in a thin tail. Only body brushes should be used, and only then after the tail has been washed.

The old-fashioned practice of strapping will not only improve the horse's coat but will also help to tone up the muscles of the neck, shoulders and hindquarters. Regular strapping can assist in muscling up a weak neck or poor hindquarters, so its benefit to the show horse can be readily appreciated. Care must be taken, though, never to strap the loins. A hay wisp, made by damping a length of hay and then twisting it into a ball, is ideal for the purpose, as are the specially made leather pads obtainable from saddlers. Fifteen to twenty minutes' daily strapping will reap its own rewards in the horse's appearance and is therefore to be recommended. Strapping should be carried out after the horse has been body brushed.

FEET AND SHOEING

Far too many people do not take enough care of their horse's feet either when the animal is young or in later life. A good farrier should attend your horse regularly every three to four weeks to keep him in good order. Clenches should be checked daily and, if any rise, knocked back down with a hammer, because if they are allowed to protrude they can easily cut a fetlock and cause a sore to develop.

If possible, youngstock should be left unshod until they are three years old as not only does this help to harden their feet but also, once they have been shod, shoeing nearly always has to be kept up. There is also the problem with youngsters that they might play about and damage themselves or spread a shoe. Nearly always it seems to happen the day before a show, necessitating the attention of the farrier who is often very difficult to get hold of at short notice. If and when you do have youngsters shod, only have light steel or aluminium plates put on in front. Some people have heavy shoes put on and then wonder why the horse or pony has lost his movement.

Riding horses require a lighter shoe than the ordinary road type. If you approach your farrier in the right manner, he will do his best for you and your animal. Obviously some farriers specialise in show-horse shoeing and are very clever at reproducing the shape of an individual horse's feet. In so doing, they dress each foot to its best advantage in helping the horse to move as level and straight as possible. I always ask my farrier to give my show hunters a slightly heavier shoe behind as, during schooling and travelling, light shoes do tend to spread. My fellow professionals will undoubtedly agree that hunters should *not* be shod with racing plates as is sometimes the case – in the hope, presumably, of helping them to move better – because they give no cover to the horses' feet on hard summer ground. This type of shoe can make them short in their stride, and there is always a danger of plates spreading and possibly cutting a fetlock.

Farrier Alan Woodyatt, winner of the Best Shod Horse competition at the Horse of the Year and Royal International Horse Shows. Correct foot dressing and shoeing is a most important part of stable management often overlooked by horse owners. Remember: 'No foot, no horse.'

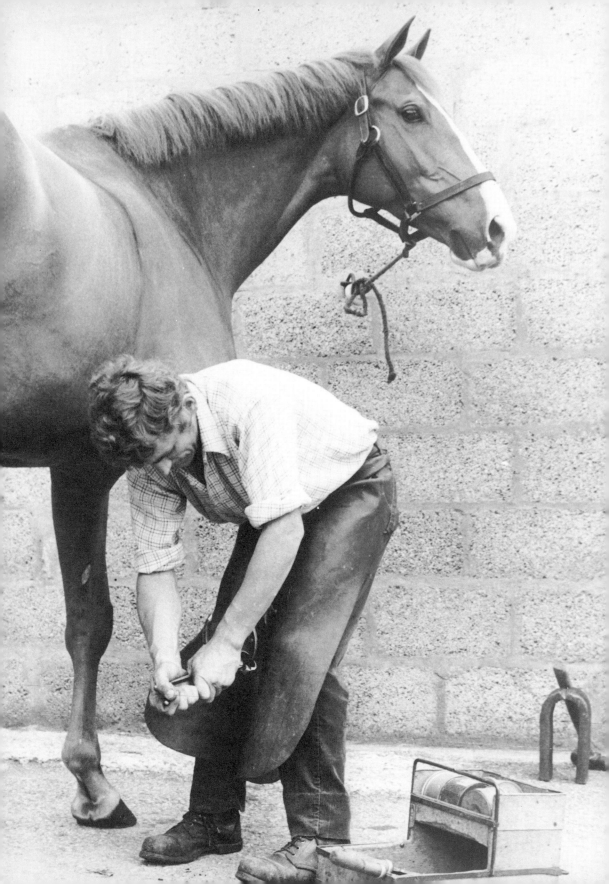

Four different types of shoe used in the show ring: top left – aluminium racing plate, suitable for hacks and ponies; top right – lightweight steel shoe suitable for most animals; bottom left – a wide aluminium shoe now used by numerous stables; bottom right – steel, mediumweight shoe most commonly used on hind feet.

Legs

In the show animal great care should be taken of the limbs at all times to protect them from wear and tear. No matter how good a horse or pony is, if he has not got clean limbs he will in all probability be called in high in his class and then, after inspection, will be placed lower down the line. Working on hard ground during the summer months makes a horse's joints fill and later may cause him to develop unsightly windgalls; many judges quite rightly put horses down which have these.

After work a show animal's legs should be washed or cleaned in the traditional way, with particular attention to the hind joints which are more prone to wear than the front ones. Apply a leg wash of one part Radiol, two parts water and one part vinegar, then dry the legs, cover them with gamgee tissue and apply a stable bandage. This helps to support the joints and keeps the legs as fine as possible. Always dry your horse's legs and heels carefully, using straw, old towels or hessian sacking. Never bandage over wet legs regularly as this will cause the hair to wrinkle and look unsightly. The bandage should never be tied tightly, particularly when travelling, as this has caused many a horse to be sent out of the ring with marked tendons.

CLIPPING AND TRIMMING

When preparing a horse or pony for ridden classes in shows early in the season, it may be necessary to clip him out to prevent loss of condition

This type of clip – a trace clip – is suitable for horses in light work. The horse shown is a four-year-old in his rough state having just been broken. Later in the year he won several good novice hack classes. Noticeably this horse lacks second thigh at this stage, but correct feeding, work and care improved this.

and so that the summer coat comes through in time. As some horses and ponies are late getting their summer coats, no amount of extra rugging etc., will enable you to get them looking right other than by clipping. Hunters should be clipped out except for their legs, while hacks, cobs and ponies are best clipped right out, legs and all. Having clipped your animal, you must ensure that he is kept really warm with two or three blankets and a night rug until his new coat comes through.

Obviously clipping has its disadvantages in that in bad weather you cannot turn clipped animals out for an hour or two to keep them sweet and calm as you would normally do. Great care must also be taken that all rugs fit properly, otherwise your horses may develop bald patches where the rugs have rubbed. Clipped animals must be groomed regularly with plenty of body brushing, or they will look starey in their coats.

Still on the question of rugs, take special care over your choice of roller, as more bad backs are caused by these than many people would ever believe. Make sure you choose a well-fitting roller with a good pad under it – many arch rollers are excellent if properly fitted. Some, however, are too narrow and tend to pinch the sides of the withers. There are a number of rug designs on the market now with the new American cross surcingles which many people find excellent for animals who slip their rugs. I have my horse's rugs fitted with back-leg straps and find these successful, particularly for youngsters which are always the worst to deal with.

One of the worst habits of young horses, which can be very difficult to cure, is ripping and chewing their rugs. One cure for the not-too-persistent offender is to make him wear an old rug with the edges painted with creosote or Cribox. Alternatively, fit a clothes bib (which you can purchase from a good saddler) to a headcollar. A bib is always a useful item in a stable as it can also be used to prevent a horse from chewing his bandages off, particularly if he is wearing them for medicinal purposes.

The heels of show animals should always be kept trimmed out either with a clipping machine or with scissors and comb, depending on the amount of hair to be removed. This does not, of course, apply to Arabs or mountain and moorland breeds. Chestnuts and ergots should always be levelled off with a sharp knife. If you are not experienced in doing this, enlist the help of someone who is.

The ears can be trimmed with either a pair of sharp scissors or a clipping machine. You can purchase portable silent clippers which are battery-charged and excellent for trimming. Opinions do differ as to the best way to clip ears, and much depends on the quality of the animal. Some have quite fluffy ears which look unattractive. Nose whiskers can be dealt with in a similar manner to the ears, and the whole look then

A bib is the most successful means of preventing a horse from chewing rugs or bandages.

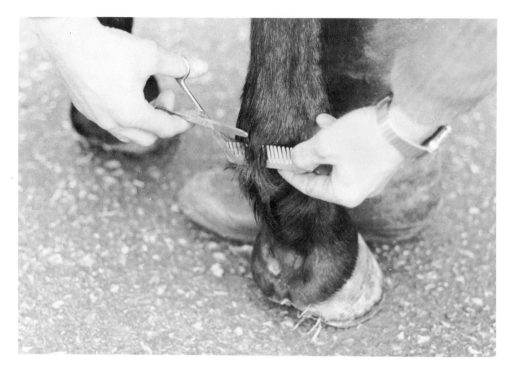

Trimming the heels with scissors and comb.

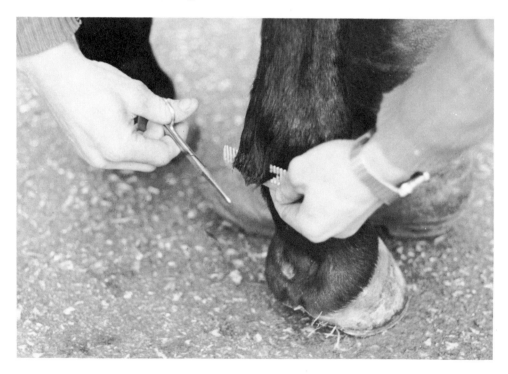

should be neat and tidy. In youngstock which spend most of their time out of doors it is advisable to leave the ears untrimmed as a protection against flies during the summer months.

TAILS

There is no doubt that a well-pulled and -shaped tail, carried correctly by its owner, is one of the most attractive parts of a horse: certainly the tail can make or mar an animal. To many people the idea of drawing hair out of the dock can be offensive or even frightening, but it is surprising what horses will suffer without objection, especially if it is carried out in a reasonable and humane way. First draw just a few hairs at a time from the sides. On no account should you attempt to take handfuls and do the job in one session: it should be carried out over a period with comb and fingers. If the animal tries to object, it is advisable to have an assistant to hold one of his front legs. Hairs both in mane and tail should be pulled straight out with a short sharp tug. The pulling of a show animal's tail is an art in itself and it is often better to get someone of experience to do it for you or at least to show you how. Particular care must be taken in the case of a fine-haired animal as it is very easy to pull out far too much hair and end up with a bald dock which will look awful for quite a long time. Never ever use a clipping machine on a tail or you will end up with disastrous results, especially as it grows, when it will resemble a loo brush!

The length of tail needs very careful judgement. Have your animal led out in hand and trotted to see if it carries its tail high or low. For hunters, riding horses and show ponies you should aim for a final length of 4 inches below the point of the hock, whether the horse is standing still or in motion. This may at first seem easy enough to achieve, but in fact it is quite the opposite. The best method is to get someone to hold the tail up in a natural position while you run your hand down the tail and, when it is in the position required, cut it parallel with the ground. For show cobs the tail can be 2–4 inches shorter.

A horse's tail should be bandaged daily to keep it in tip-top condition. The bandage can be applied after grooming and left on for between one and four hours. On no account should it be kept bandaged for exceptionally long periods, however, as this can cause soreness and loss of hair. Many a horse or pony has lost its tail through tight bandaging and, in particular, tight tapes. Never wet the bandage, but always damp the top of the tail. The new elastic bandages available now are excellent for the job.

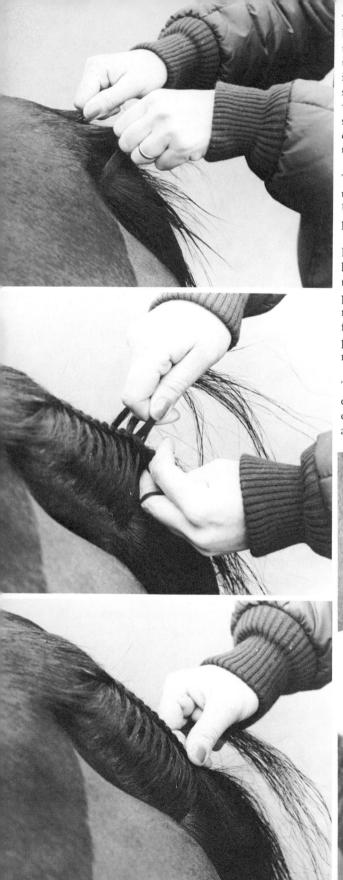

Tail plaiting. Before you begin, the tail must be well brushed, clean and free of grease and tangles. Having wet the tail well, take a section of hair from either side of the tail (one in each hand). With the left hand pick up a small section of hair from the centre. You will now have three strands from which to start plaiting. (N.B. The form of plaiting demonstrated requires that the strands are taken *under* not over to form the plait.)

Take the piece of hair in your right hand under the centre section, plait and pull tight. Use your right thumb to hold the plait in place.

Next, with your left hand take a section of hair from the left-hand side and bring that to the centre and plait under. Secure the plait with your left thumb. Then, use your right hand to take in a small section of hair from the right-hand side of the tail, and repeat the above procedure, plaiting until you reach the end of the dock.

The hair taken from the sides must be of even size and not too thick, and the secret of good plaiting is to keep the work as tight as possible.

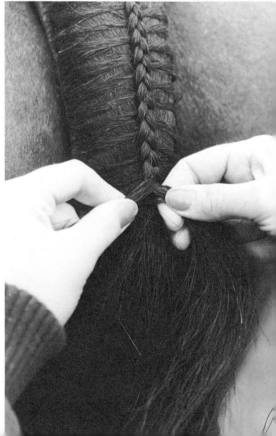

above, *left*   When you reach the end of the dock, make one long plait of the three strands of hair you have left.

above, *right*   Take a needle and thread and sew the end of the plait tightly by overstitching. Make a large loop, as shown, tuck the end under the main plaited section and secure with thread. Then continue stitching down the pigtail, joining the two sides, to make it lie flat. Finish off with a secure knot.

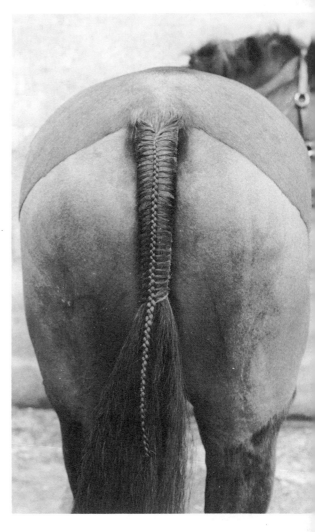

right   The finished tail.

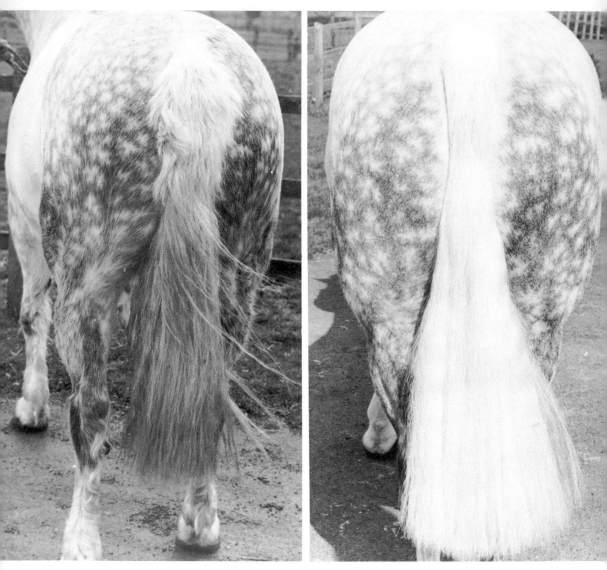

left An unruly tail in need of attention. *right* The same tail after correct pulling, washing and bandaging. For the show ring it should be shortened so that it is 2 inches lower than the point of the hock.

In youngstock classes, you can plait your animal's tail if you wish. In fact there are no rules to stop you showing any horse with a plaited tail (except, of course, native breeds), but in ridden classes it is the practice always to pull the tail.

Manes

Manes should not be over-pulled or shortened, otherwise as the season goes on you may well find that you are becoming short of mane as a result of the constant plaiting and unplaiting. The number of plaits can vary according to the individual animal's conformation and head carriage. The old way of seven or nine has long gone out of fashion and it is not unusual to see as many as twenty tiny plaits. In my opinion this is rather ridiculous, especially if they are put in with coloured rubber bands.

Hunters, however, look best with about ten to twelve neat plaits well sewn with thread. Hacks' and ponies' appearance can be enhanced with about the same number and, if needed, a couple more, very small and neat and well stitched in. Obviously, if your animal has a short, thick neck, it will require a greater number of plaits to make it look better. Trial and error at home will show you the best number for your horse

Mane pulling. Take a handful of hair between finger and thumb, and use a comb to push up (back-comb) surplus hair until only a few long hairs remain. Twist these hairs around the comb and draw them out. Manes should be thinned gradually over a period of days to avoid soreness. Finish by damping the mane to encourage it to lie flat.

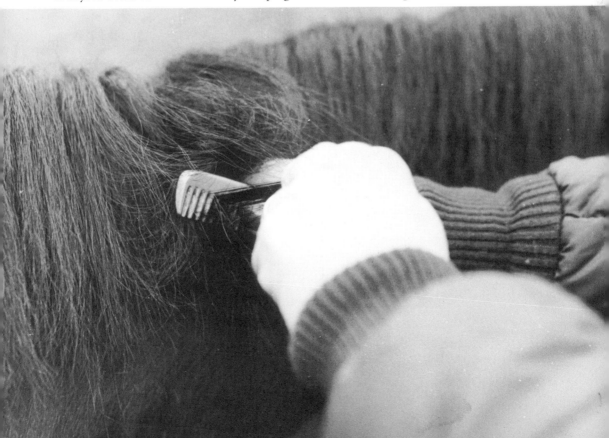

or pony – it is worth taking the trouble to find out as a great deal of difference to a horse's appearance can be made with good plaiting.

The section at the top of the mane where the bridle headpiece goes can, if you wish, be cut out about an inch, but on no account should any more be removed – as is often done – or by the time you have taken a large slice of the top and the same from the withers, you will have room for only about four plaits in the middle. If you buy a horse or pony which has been mutilated in this way, you will unfortunately have to bear with the problem during the year of purchase. Allow the hair to grow out during the following winter and all will probably be well again by the next season. This rule, of course, also applies if your hand strayed into the mane while clipping, leaving an ugly row of cut hair.

If you decide to hog your horse's mane bear in mind that you will have to clip it once a week during the show season to keep it looking really good. When using the clippers on the mane take care not to clip into the horse's coat.

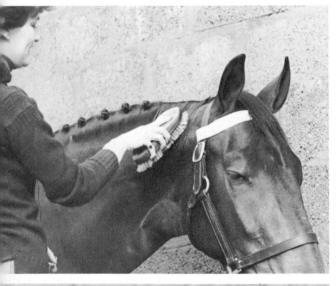

Mane plaiting. Always wet the mane well. Having worked out the number of plaits you want, you can either begin at the top of the neck, which is the more conventional starting place, or at the withers. You can measure out the plaits with an ordinary nylon hair comb cut to a length that will produce the size of plaits to suit your horse. Trial and error will determine the right length for the comb.

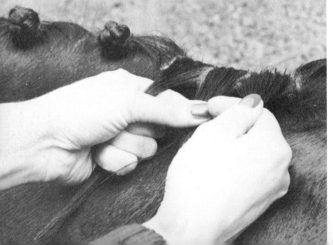

Divide the section of hair into three equal pieces. Use a comb to keep unwanted hair out of the way.

Plait very tightly together.

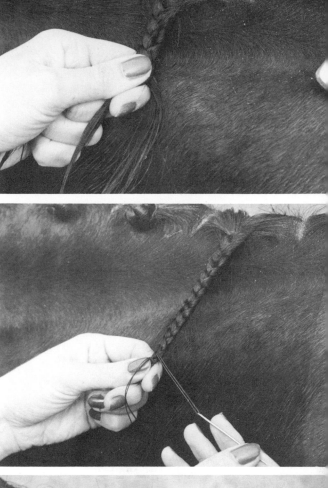

Secure the end of the plait with thread.

Take the end of the plait up to the base of the mane and put a stitch in it. For extra security you can take the thread once round the base of the plait.

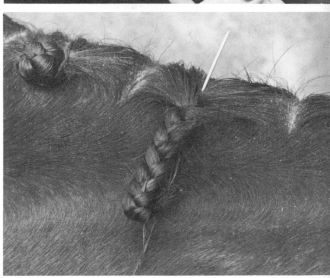

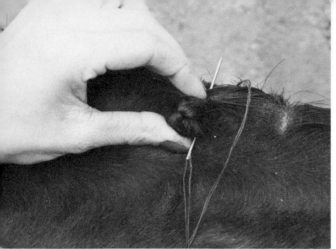

Double up once or twice more, depending on the length of plait, and stitch tight.

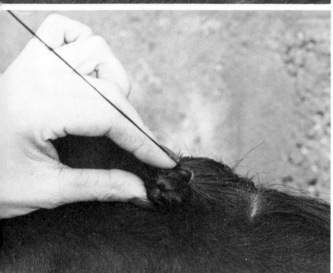

Finish by passing the thread round the base of the plait and sewing through the plait two or three times, keeping the stitches small and neat. Do not be tempted to trim away any stray hairs as to do so will lead to problems in the future.

below The final look of a well-plaited mane. When unplaiting take care not to snip any hair accidentally.

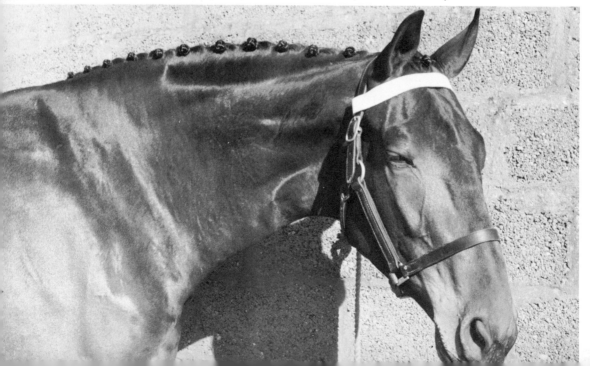

SHAMPOOING

Many people of the old school of thought were aghast at the thought of washing horses, but today it seems to have been accepted as a matter of course. To shampoo a stabled horse is beneficial to health and appearance, provided great care is taken over drying, particularly in winter. I personally have shampooed show horses for many years now and none of them has experienced any detrimental effects either in the form of colds or cracked heels. While there is no substitute for correct grooming and strapping, washing certainly has its uses and, of course, in grey animals it is essential to wash in order to remove stable stains.

The best time to shampoo horses and ponies is before or after clipping. It removes all surplus grease and dirt, leaving the coat clean and healthy. Use your common sense, though: do not get an animal out of the field

below, *left* Shampooing is a regular practice in show yards. *below*, *right* Use of the hose pipe is not always practicable but if it *is* used take care not to frighten the horse.

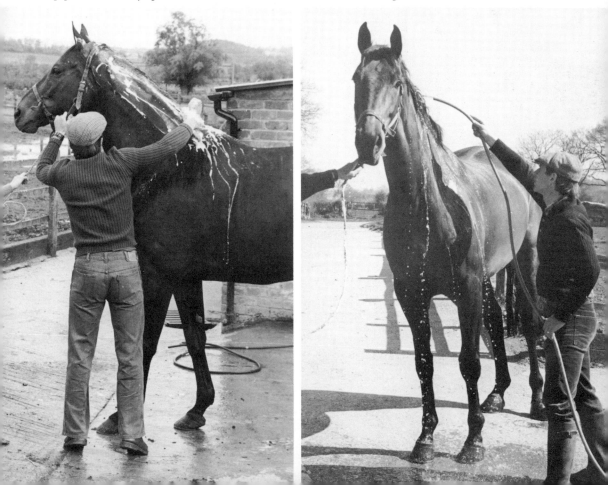

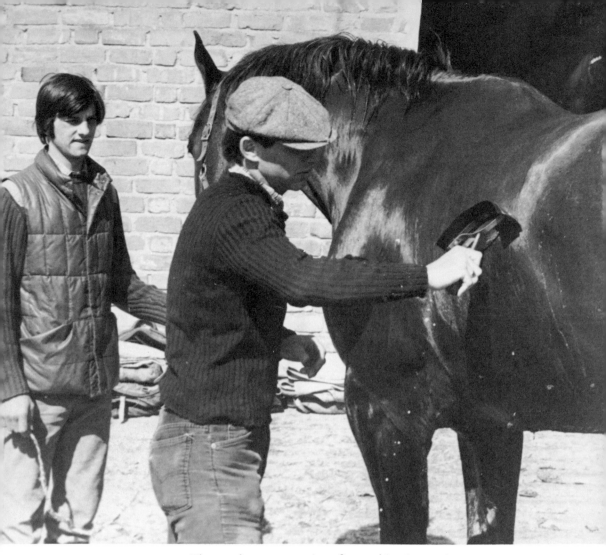

Thorough sweat-scraping after washing is very important.

one day, shampoo it, take part in a competition, then on return put it straight back out. This is the way to make your horse catch a chill.

Washing should, if possible, be carried out in a spare box some yards away from your horse's usual stable. Even better, have a wash box, specially kitted out. If, however, you can manage neither of these, washing can easily be done outside with someone holding the horse.

Start by wetting the animal all over, then apply one of the many brands of animal shampoo, paying particular attention to the mane and tail. Then, using either a hose pipe or buckets, swill all excess shampoo from the coat. The next most important thing is to get the animal dry as soon as possible. In sunny weather this is no problem; on cooler days you can lunge your horse until he is dry, or dry him with straw and stable rubbers and finish by bandaging his legs and putting on several spare rugs.

7

Tack and Equipment

The most important items of tack for the show horse or pony are the saddle and bridle. To start with, many people buy inferior-quality tack, and whilst this may be acceptable for local shows, if you want to do the job properly and follow in the footsteps of the professionals you must have the most correct tack you can possibly acquire.

For any show class in which the judge has to ride your horse or pony, it is of the utmost importance that the saddle fits the animal correctly. To determine whether a saddle fits, it must be tested with someone sitting on it. Remember to avoid unnecessarily padded panels in a saddle, because the closer you are to the horse, the better you will ride and the firmer your grip will be. There is nothing more comforting than to sit well into a horse on a good saddle.

Remember, too, that it is a great mistake to appear in the ring in brand-new light-coloured tack. It should be well oiled and darkened. In this connection, bear in mind that neatsfoot oil does not rot tack as is often thought.

HUNTERS

Hopefully your hunter will be acquainted with a plain double bridle, for this is what he should be shown in. An average short-cheeked weymouth is what most horses go best in. Opt for stainless-steel bits, which not only look better but also are less likely to break or bend than cheap nickel ones. Whether you prefer billet stud ends or stitched reins is a personal choice. The cheek pieces on your hunter's bridle should be threequarters of an inch wide as nothing looks or feels worse to a judge than narrow, flimsy leather. The reins should be threequarters of an inch wide for the top rein and half an inch wide for the bottom one. Coloured browbands should never be seen on hunters, under any circumstances, and plain leather nosebands are preferable to stitched ones. If your horse has a plain head, a good wide noseband specially made for you by your saddler will help to cover his plainness. Obviously you must be governed by your own judgment as to the weight class of your horse and to the size of his head.

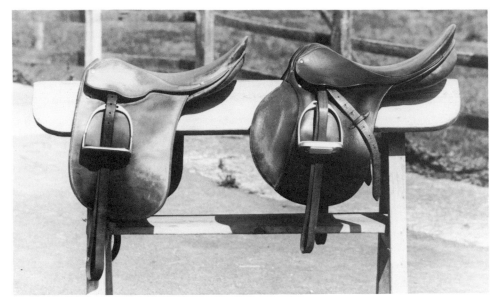

The suede-covered saddle on the left would be suitable for a wide range of horses in the show ring. On the right is a nice type of general-purpose saddle ideal for schooling and working hunters.

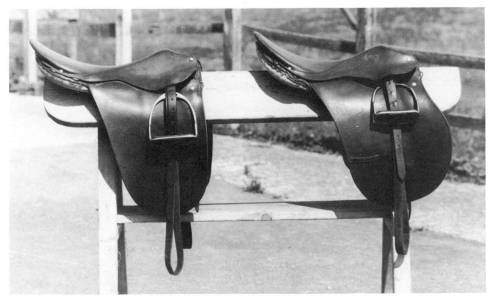

Two fine examples of Owen saddles that should fit most animals comfortably without the use of a numnah. On the left is a straight-cut saddle more suitable for a hack; the saddle on the right is slightly forward cut to suit a cob, riding horse or hunter.

You are allowed to show in any type of bit you wish. Some horses go well in a pelham. The aim, of course, is that your animal should go quietly and with a still head carriage. You also have a choice of various lengths of curb bits, depending on the severity you want. A heavyweight show hunter will in all probability need a much longer curb bit than a lightweight four-year-old. Only trial and error will show you what is right for you and your horse. An important point always to bear in mind with any animal in the ring is that when you get as many as twenty galloping together, it is very different from riding alone at home.

If you are lucky, you may have an old hunting-weight double bridle at home or may possibly be able to borrow one from a friend until you

Master Kempley, a thoroughbred brown gelding. He was Lightweight Show Hunter of the Year in 1975 and afterwards won many working-hunter classes. Here he is seen in perfect show condition and suitably equipped for any working-hunter class. The rider is correctly dressed for hunter classes except that the spurs are worn too low – this is a common fault which is often overlooked.

are sure as to which type suits your particular horse. When buying a new bridle, be sure to go to a reputable saddler. Take special care to purchase a bit of the correct size: a common error is to get one that is far too wide. When fitting a double bridle, have it high enough in the horse's mouth so that it just crinkles the lips. Far too many people allow them to hang too low and then wonder why the animal has its tongue over the bit. To finish off, you have a choice of curb chains, depending again on your animal. You may need a chain-leather or, for novices and four-year-olds, an elastic one. A lip strap is useful to keep the curb in the right place.

In hunter classes especially, a good second-hand hunting saddle made by a reputable firm such as Owen, Champion and Wilton or Whippy is excellent if you can get hold of one. When purchasing a second-hand saddle, get the saddler to examine the tree for soundness, because in some old saddles the tree may have cracked and spread. A show saddle to avoid is a cheaply made straight-cut one that is uncomfortable to sit on; such saddles rarely fit the animal anyway. Several leading saddlers in Britain are now marketing their own type, often based on the old pattern, and I have tried a few and found them satisfactory.

WORKING HUNTERS

In working-hunter classes you are allowed any type of bridle, plus a martingale of your own choice. It is up to you to fit the bridle your horse goes best in, but ideally you should have a plain double or snaffle with possibly a running martingale.

The saddle can again be the old hunting type, if this best suits your purpose.

HACKS

A show hack is allowed a finely made bridle with a stitched noseband, together with a coloured browband. For this, velvet ribbon in two contrasting colours is the best material, and it can be home-made or purchased from a good saddler. Plastic ones are often frowned upon, but again you are free to choose what you like best. Your hack bridle reins need to be made of half- to threequarter-inch leather. Do not have them made so fine, as some people do, that to a judge holding them on a wet day they appear like pieces of string. As with the hunter, a hack is allowed to have

Tenterk, a 15.2 hh thoroughbred gelding by Tenderhooks, owned and bred by Mrs D. Goodall. Tenterk became Champion Show Hack in three consecutive years at the Horse of the Year Show. His correct conformation, movement and ride made him virtually unbeatable. He is shown here wearing suitable tack for hack classes.

any type of pelham or double in which it goes best. Neatness and simplicity are what is needed where hack bridles are concerned.

It is most important when showing hacks that not only does the saddle fit the animal correctly but, where leathers and irons are concerned, you also bear in mind that a large man may be judging. Whatever class you are competing in, if you are a small woman or girl, have a groom bring you in a spare large pair of leathers and irons. When choosing a hack saddle, avoid the too-straight-cut front and short tree. To a judge, they feel as if they are about to slip over the front and also give no proper feel of the horse's ride. Some reversed-hide (suede) show saddles, if made large enough, are quite good. Ideally all show saddles should be lined in serge or linen, particularly for hacks that are thin-skinned (hunters and cobs can tolerate a leather lining). In hack classes if you have a leather-lined saddle, a small sheepskin numnah is quite permissible. Do avoid large, fluffy, coloured ones: if you can get hold of one, a black sheepskin is ideal. Have all numnahs trimmed to the size of your saddle: nothing looks worse than to see two inches of sheepskin showing round the edge.

RIDING HORSES

The correct tack for the show riding horse is a double bridle or pelham fitted with a coloured browband and stitched noseband if you wish. The size of the bridle depends on the type of riding horse you have – hack or hunter – and should correspond with the size of the horse's head. Any type of saddle is permissible for the show riding horse provided it fits and is comfortable to ride in.

COBS

With show cobs you have to 'bridle the head', as the professionals say. This means that if your cob has a plain head, fit a strong, thick bridle with the noseband one and a half to two inches wide. Nothing looks worse than a plain head wearing a narrow, fancy bridle. Cobs always look better with a heavyweight bridle and a plain hunting saddle. The problem with most cobs is that they are usually wide across the withers and it is difficult getting a saddle to fit close enough – and remember, when showing, that the saddle makes all the difference to the ride. You can always ask your saddler to take some of the stuffing out of your saddle to make it fit your cob correctly. Usually he will be only too happy to oblige if allowed enough time. If you are having a saddle made, tell him it is for a wide show cob and he will probably be pleased to measure it up from your own animal. In any case it makes sense, when having any new saddle made, to have a proper fitting before it is finished.

SHOW PONIES

Show ponies, with the exception of novices, should always be shown in a pelham or double bridle depending on which your pony goes best in. A narrow leather bridle with the bits stitched on looks the neatest. Have

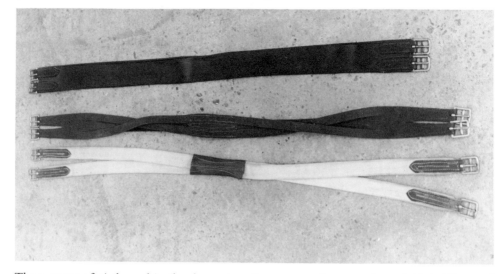

Three types of girth used in the show ring. From top to bottom: three-fold, balding and canvas show girth.

a stitched noseband but remember that if your pony has a long or broad head, a plain cavesson noseband will help to cover up this fault. The bits should always be stainless steel, both for looks and safety. A nicely made, coloured velvet browband looks very effective. On novice, first-ridden and leading-rein ponies, a snaffle is required. On lead-rein ponies the rein must be fixed on to the noseband. Care must always be taken when fixing the curb chain. It must lie flat with the centre rings hanging down so that the lip strap can go through smoothly: not surprisingly, show ponies sometimes do not go well when the curb chain is twisted. Any type of curb is permitted, so choose one that your pony goes best in.

When selecting a saddle, remember that many ponies are flat on their withers. A good secondhand one may have the advantage that it fits your pony better than a new one as it is already broken in. Avoid the very straight-cut saddle with a flat seat as a young person will find it difficult to sit on.

Working–hunter Ponies

In all working-hunter pony classes, the choice of tack is left to the individual, so fit your pony with a bridle that he jumps well in. A running martingale is permissible in this class, as are general-purpose jumping saddles. No coloured browbands may be used. The whole outfit should give pony and rider the appearance of being able to last a day's hunting in any country and do some work while looking neat and tidy.

In-hand Classes

In all in-hand showing classes it is advisable to have a bit in the animal's mouth – even a yearling – because the sight and sound of modern showgrounds can make even the quietest animal take fright. There are many good examples of in-hand bridles at all the leading saddlers.

Young hunters in hand can, if you wish, have a headcollar fitted with a browband and with a bit attached. In three-year-old classes a double bridle is in order, but do remember that if your animal plays up you only have the length of rein to hold on to, and if it rears it will very likely get loose. It's best, therefore, to use one only if you are sure of your young horse's manners.

A straight bar snaffle is best for a young animal as it is less likely to get its tongue over it – the worst habit any young horse can get into and the reason that so many prize-winning youngsters never go on to win in later life; their mouths have been ruined by badly fitted bridles and when ridden they have no proper mouth but are often one-sided. You can now purchase nylon-covered straight bar bits which are ideal for youngstock. You must avoid wide, broken snaffles hanging out of their mouths. Remember never to jab youngsters in the mouth as this bruises and deadens the bars of the mouth. Have a coupling fitted to both sides of the bit as again this gives a more level bearing on the mouth.

Lead reins can be of leather or webbing and of a length and width of your choice. Bear in mind, however, that a wet leather one can easily slip through your hand and you could find your valuable young animal galloping loose around the show ring, possibly with disastrous results. Never run a chain through the two rings on a bit, as some exhibitors do, to show a young animal: this is far too severe and only makes the horse or pony afraid to come up level to the handler. It is, after all, the art of in-hand showing to have your animal level with you but well behaved.

All brood mares shown in hand should be fitted with a double bridle of the same pattern and type they would need if they were being ridden. Foals should wear foal slips and, if necessary, browbands can be fitted. If your foal is rather plain, a white browband does help to brighten it up and make it more attractive.

SIDESADDLES

Although there are a few new sidesaddles coming on to the market, most of the saddles around today are secondhand. If you can find a good secondhand one, perhaps made by firms such as Champion and Wilton, Owen or Mayhew, you will do better than buying a cheap, new version. Sidesaddles can cost as much as £1000 with £500 being about average, so beware of one with a very low price tag.

Buying secondhand tack is a tricky business so first-time buyers should seek expert advice from their saddler (if he has experience with side-saddles), the Sidesaddle Association or a prominent showing person. Side-saddles used to be made to measure; it is therefore important to check that any intended purchase fits both horse and rider. When buying, avoid the old-fashioned *very* heavy hunting saddles as these are really too weighty even if made by a reputable firm.

If you do go in for sidesaddle riding take special care when transporting your tack: sidesaddles are easily damaged because of their awkward shape.

GADGETS AND ARTIFICIAL AIDS

When producing horses and ponies for the show ring, there will come a time when you encounter a difficult animal which does not settle in its mouth and you will have the problem of finding the bit that it goes best in. For animals to be shown in classes where they have to be ridden by the judge, this is obviously more difficult, whether your animal is light-mouthed or very strong.

The light-mouthed horse or pony may do best with a rubber pelham fitted with an elastic curb chain. If this does not suit him, try a broken-mouthed vulcanite or steel pelham. A straight-barred pelham covered in chamois leather will also often work wonders.

With horses that are strong, it is more difficult to tell at home if you have chosen the best bit than it is in the ring among other animals galloping. Try a long-cheeked curb first, and if this is not successful try a high port in the curb bit. A Banbury curb with a sliding cheek can also be effective. Several of the pelham bits with long cheeks often have the desired effect, particularly the Rugby pelham.

It is always best to get experienced help with any bitting problems. You should also, of course, always check that the animal has no teeth problems or sore gums, because however many different bits you try you will never cure an animal that is not medically right in its mouth. Remember that horses and ponies pull for many reasons: natural excitement, too much corn, ring craftiness, bad bitting and, last but not least, a nervous rider. Many people think that a horse is particularly stupid to pull against the rider as this causes the animal himself discomfort, but often the more the rider pulls on the reins, the more the horse will pull against the rider. Holding a strong horse is a knack rather than a sign of strength in the rider, as can be seen from the fact that very strong race-horses are often held by small lads. In the ring a sympathetic give and take on the rein will often have the desired effect. Many people actually encourage their horses to pull and run away in the ring by over-galloping them – they let them gallop flat out at two or three shows which soon teaches them to pull and run on. It is surprising how often riders, when showing a puller, say that they have given the horse a good gallop the day before to take the steam out of him. This is absurd because it only teaches such horses to pull more. The more you gallop some animals, the more they will pull; you will simply end up turning them into confirmed pullers.

Tack Cleaning

All leather tack should be regularly cleaned and oiled to keep it supple and strong. Cleaning tack provides a good opportunity to check for signs of wear and tear. To neglect your tack is to neglect yourself and your horse – not only is it dangerous to ride with faulty tack but also dirty tack can lead to skin sores on the horse. Taking a little extra care over the cleaning and maintenance of your tack will reap its own rewards in the show ring.

Leather tack should first be washed with a sponge to remove any dirt and grease. There is simply no point applying saddle soap or polish unless this washing is carried out thoroughly. 'Jockeys', small accumulations of dirt and grease often seen on the saddle flaps, can be removed with a small ball of plaited horsehair and warm water. Once the leather is dry apply saddle soap – the clear glycerine bar type is best – using a damp, clean sponge and paying attention to both sides of the leather where this is accessible. Try not to apply too much soap, especially on saddles as this could have disastrous effects on your breeches.

After saddle-soaping hang the tack up in a cool, airy place to dry. On no account should it be left by a fire or any other source of heat. There is no need to finish off by buffing with a cloth.

Your tack will benefit from a periodic dressing of neatsfoot oil. About once every two months should be about right.

A well-equipped, tidy tack-room. However, saddles should never be placed on top of one another as this can cause the trees to spread.

When preparing for a show clean your tack at least one day in advance to give it time to dry. To make the tack sparkle, polish up the buckles with Brasso or similar metal polish. Apply the polish after the tack has been washed but before saddle-soaping. Incidentally, buckles should be opened and oiled from time to time to keep them in good order.

Linen-lined saddles can be whitened, but this is unnecessary and, to my mind, excessive – all sorts of problems arise if the linen gets wet and the whitener starts to run. Areas of suede or reversed hide on saddles can be smartened up with a stiff brush.

8

Dress

There are many rules, both written and unwritten, about the correct attire for riding, and it never ceases to amaze me how people unwittingly spoil their appearance – and therefore also their chances in the show ring – by wearing unsuitable clothes. It has been said that the best-dressed person is the one whose clothes attract the least attention. Garments should be of good quality and fit the wearer well but need not necessarily be new or expensive. Even very old clothes can look extremely presentable if well cleaned and properly worn; in fact, some old coats and boots are of a much higher quality than those made today and are much sought after.

If you can afford it, go to a well-known outfitter. This may mean extra expense initially, but your clothes will fit better and the good-quality materials from which they are made will obviously be more durable. Clothes which are incorrect or ill-fitting will be uncomfortable and cause you dissatisfaction, if not even embarrassment! The rider who is correctly dressed and looks workmanlike will certainly have the advantage over someone who is either too scruffy or flashily dressed when it comes to making an impression in the show ring. Bear in mind this poem by Egerton Warburtons:

> Tain't the coat that makes the rider,
> Leathers, boots, nor yet the cap.
> They who come their coat to show,
> They better were at home in bed.
> What of hunting and horses know they?
> Nothing else but go ahead.

Clothing for Ridden Classes

In the classes for ridden and working hunters, hacks, cobs and riding horses, the general rule is that ladies and gentlemen wear ratcatcher, this being a hunting term which describes the correct dress for cub hunting. The coat should be a well-cut hacking jacket with either one or two vents at the back. There are many choices of material and colour, but the smartest will usually be a fairly plain tweed, so try not to pick a coat with too gaudy a check. Nowadays it is possible to buy good-quality coats ready made and these will be perfectly acceptable. Ideally, though, a jacket will be made to measure, and if you are prepared to go to this expense do make sure it is cut with a fitting waist, a full skirt and rather longer than an ordinary sports coat. Ladies may, if they prefer, wear a blue or black hunting coat in these classes.

Breeches for ladies and gentlemen can be in any colour the individual prefers, ranging from brown to canary yellow, except white. There is a wide range of materials from which to choose and some of the ready-made stretch breeches are very reasonably priced. The new fabrics are lighter and are often far more comfortable than the traditional materials, especially on a hot day. Ladies should avoid wearing brightly patterned underwear under light coloured breeches – it may catch the judge's eye but it is not considered elegant. If you want to be really smart, it is hard to better a pair of hand-made lightweight cavalry-twill breeches which, with the proper care, will last many years.

Moving on to shirts and ties, there is once again a wide range of colours and styles in all sizes from which to choose. The main criterion is neatness, so a plain shirt or one with a neat check is quite suitable for both ladies and gentlemen. With many professional riders these days, a blue striped shirt with a white collar finds favour. A blue spotted tie gives the finished look, but again a plain colour is quite permissible.

There are no hard-and-fast rules when it comes to the type of glove to be worn, but probably the smartest and most suitable would be a pair of good-quality tan pigskin. On a rainy day it would be sensible to change to a pair of yellow string gloves, because leather on wet reins becomes extremely slippery and horses can take advantage of this when galloping on. Black evening-dress-type gloves do not look good worn in the ring: they are as out of place as pigskin gloves would be at a dance.

Ladies have the option of wearing a hunting cap or a bowler. Although by tradition it is considered that the bowler is correct attire, either would be acceptable in the ring. Gentlemen, however, have no choice and the official headwear for ratcatcher is the bowler hat. It is most important to purchase one's hunting cap or bowler from a leading outfitter who knows the correct fit and the style in which it should be worn, for nothing looks worse than a hat perched on the back of the head. There has been a great deal of public concern and debate over the safety aspect of hats and space does not permit further commentary here. If you buy the best quality that you can afford and make sure it fits well, you should be safe.

Showing whips come in many shapes and sizes. At one end of the scale you can cut a holly stick and dry it until seasoned or, at the other extreme, you can buy an expensive antique whip adorned with silver. The ideal to help you 'look the part' in a show is a nice cane covered in leather and of a size to suit you. One occasionally sees the cheap, long schooling whips, but these are frowned upon and look out of place in the ring.

The final item of riding wear is probably the most important, for boots can make or mar the overall appearance of horse and rider. Nothing looks smarter than a highly polished pair of well-fitting black boots, but equally nothing looks worse than scruffy or ill-fitting ones. The usual colour for the show ring is black, although brown boots are occasionally seen and are considered perfectly correct when worn with a grey bowler hat. The ideal would be to have a pair of hand-made black boots of waxed-calf or box-calf leather which, although they would probably be the most expensive item in a riding outfit, should with proper care last a lifetime. If you are going to have boots made for you, make sure that they are long enough to come right up to the bottom of the knee as they are bound to drop a little with wear. There is, of course, no point in having good boots made without specially fitted trees, and these can be very expensive. If you can't afford trees then stuff the boots with newspaper to help them keep their shape and prevent wrinkling.

When cleaning leather boots you should apply two coats of black polish, bringing up a shine with a soft rag. As with tack, sponge the boots with water first to remove any mud and horse grease, and allow them to dry before putting on polish. If the boots are of waxed calf they can be boned, which forces the polish right into the surface of the leather. If possible use the shin bone of a deer, obtainable from a reputable London bootmaker. Apply the bone in a downward direction for the foot, and an upward direction for the leg. Finish off with a final coating of shoe cream and buff up to a high gloss.

Nowadays there are plenty of ready-made riding boots available and many of them are very good value. These are obviously more practical for the young person who is still growing or for day-to-day wear. A lot of people have taken to wearing rubber boots in the ring and these can look quite presentable if they are cleaned with ordinary boot polish. They are very useful in the wet conditions which sometimes have to be borne. Some people get their saddler to fit their rubber boots with patent-leather tops, which makes them look smart.

To finish off the correct look, you will need a pair of garter straps which are attached to the tops of the boots. You should be sure that they are fitted between the second and third button of your breeches and that the tongue of each strap is on the outside. If your breeches do not have buttons, you should sew two on each leg so that the garter straps can be fitted correctly.

Finally you will need a pair of spurs. These are officially part of the correct dress, but whether they are worn or not is up to the individual rider and the horse. There are many different patterns of spurs with a varying length of neck, but ideally for the show ring you should have a neat, plain spur with a short neck which is always worn facing down. Very occasionally a sluggish horse may need a reminder with a slightly harsher spur with a longer neck, but on no account should spurs with rowlers be used in the ring.

Dress for Special Performances at Major Shows

All the items of dress discussed so far would be suitable for any show class except for the afternoon and evening performances at the Royal International Horse Show or the Horse of the Year Show. When competing at either of these shows, there is a further set of rules regarding dress to follow.

In the hunter classes gentlemen are expected to wear full hunting costume which includes a silk top hat and hunting tie or stock, as it is often called. (The late Duke of Beaufort had very strong views about this and always insisted on their being referred to as ties because, as he so rightly reminded us, a stock is part of a gun.) Gloves, white or yellow breeches and a pair of top boots (i.e. black with mahogany tops), garter straps and spurs are also required apparel. For these occasions gentlemen can wear a red coat which can either be swallow-tailed or the traditional frock style. Please do not describe these coats as 'pink' because Pink was simply the name of the fashionable tailor who used to make them many years ago. The colour may be referred to as scarlet if you wish; this is the term used by hunt servants. There is a tale about a young man who went to hunt in Warwickshire with the late Lord Willoughby de Broke, and on asking his lordship if he could wear his pink coat he received the reply, 'Wear yellow knickers if you want, but I personally always wear a red coat.'

A black frock or swallow-tail coat would be equally correct but not quite so smart for a gentleman. The black coat should be accompanied

Vin Toulson wearing correct dress for a final cob and hunter class at Horse of the Year or Royal International Horse Shows. This outfit, which would be equally correct out hunting, consists of silk top hat, hunting tie (stock), black cut-away coat, pigskin gloves, hunting whip, black boots with patent tops and spurs, yellow waistcoat and yellow breeches.

by fawn or yellow breeches and plain black boots. To finish the picture, a hunting whip should be carried – once again, this is the correct name, not 'crop'.

Ladies have the choice of wearing a silk top hat or a bowler. They would be correctly attired in a blue or black coat and any colour of breeches, with black boots and spurs. They may carry an ordinary cane. Both ladies and gentlemen should, of course, always wear a waistcoat and this may be of any colour or material. The bottom button should be left undone.

In these special performances the correct attire for ladies in hack classes is the same as has been described for hunters, the only addition being a small flower in the buttonhole to give a finishing touch. The gentlemen in the hack classes should wear a silk top hat, a black coat made on the same lines as a morning coat, a cravat or collar and tie, black close-fitting riding trousers and dress spurs if desired. A cane should be carried by ladies and gentlemen.

Anyone who has seen the evening performances of the hunters and hacks under the spotlights at these two great shows would agree that this formal dress makes for a very splendid sight indeed.

In-hand Showing Clothes

There are no hard-and-fast rules with regard to clothes for any in-hand showing classes. It is more or less left to the individual to decide what to wear. One has to be practical and, of course, much will depend on the weather on the day: this is a point to bear in mind when packing to go to a show away from home.

Ladies can vary their appearance from the very practical and unadorned to full regalia of smart dress and hat. Gentlemen, on the other hand, to be correct, should wear a suit or sports coat with smart trousers together with polished boots or shoes. They should always wear a bowler hat and carry a stick, the whole outfit looking neat and tidy.

Writing this reminds me of my friend the late Harry Jarret, who for so many years was stud groom to Norman Crow of Shropshire. In his smart brown suit, bowler hat and polished lace-up boots, Harry had many admirers. He was also, incidentally, the best man I have ever seen showing a young hunter. It was often said that Harry did not need a horse to win a prize but that to walk into the ring with his highly polished in-hand bridle would be sufficient! He was one of the old school of stud grooms

Turnout for in-hand classes is equally as important as in ridden classes. On the right is the late Harry Jarret who exemplified this principle; on the left is Mr E. E. Griffiths with the author in the centre.

whom we miss today. Their knowledge was based on a lifetime's experience of working with many different types of horse: not only of handling them but also caring for them and attending to their well-being. Luckily we have Harry's son, Gordon, carrying on in his father's footsteps.

GROOMS' CLOTHING

Grooms should be neat and tidy in their appearance when attending horses in the ring. They should also always wear a hard hat when exercising on showgrounds as this is a time when accidents can happen. This piece of necessary apparel should be paid for by their employers.

CHILDREN'S SHOW CLASSES

Children's clothes for the ring do not vary very much from the local show to the Horse of the Year Show. Boys look smart in tweed coats at local and county shows. Remember that the turnout of riders, particularly in children's classes, counts for a great deal. A neat child beautifully turned out in a large class of ponies is readily noticed. Judges are often able to pick out the different ponies in very large classes by what the child is wearing. For the larger shows a blue or black jacket is more appropriate, together with a well-made close-fitting pair of jodhpurs – you can now purchase very smart ready-made ones for any age of child.

Proper jodhpur boots that fit well should be worn. An important point to remember with all riding boots is that, when repair is required, the cobbler should be asked to take the new sole through to the heel. If it is made short, there is always the risk that, in the case of a fall, the new short sole could get caught in the stirrup iron and the rider dragged as a result. Black or brown boots are both permissible. Long black boots are only occasionally worn by children in their last year, but they can make the wearers look too old for their class. Spurs, of course, are rightly never allowed in any children's pony classes.

A neat leather-covered cane with a pair of woollen or leather gloves completes the ensemble, plus a well-fitting riding hat. The hat makes a considerable difference to the overall appearance of a child rider.

Some parents dress their children in matching coats and hats. These can look smart, but it does depend on the colour of the pony. The main aim should be neatness and cleanliness in the whole outfit: this is what really counts at the end of the day.

LADIES' SIDESADDLE

Almost everyone will agree that a lady riding sidesaddle and correctly turned out is the most delightful sight on the equestrian scene. The object of sidesaddle turnout is for the rider to look elegant and extremely neat and tidy – just as if she had stepped out of a Munnings painting.

The correct dress for a lady showing either a hack or a hunter sidesaddle before noon is a bowler hat, veil, navy, black or tweed habit, collar and tie and woollen or pigskin gloves. Black nylon or twill breeches are correct, but some prefer to wear their fawn-coloured ones which cannot be seen when they are mounted. Hair should always be kept tied back and covered by a net. If your hair is long enough to be worn in a bun, so much the better; if not, wear a false bun. Earrings should never be

Horse and rider suitably dressed for a sidesaddle class. Special care must be taken in the turnout of sidesaddle classes otherwise they can resemble Mad Hatter's tea parties!

worn as they are considered very incorrect. (Remember that this rule applies to hunting too.) After noon it is considered correct etiquette to put on a top hat, veil and white hunting tie (*not* a stock).

Hunting ties should be tied really tight with a small knot and well pinned with a plain gold pin (avoid horses and foxes' masks, etc.) Nothing looks worse on a lady – or gentlemen – than a loose, floppy tie. Everyone has their own ideas as to how they should be tied, so use your own method and when buying choose a neat, fine, half-silk one as you will find this easier to tie.

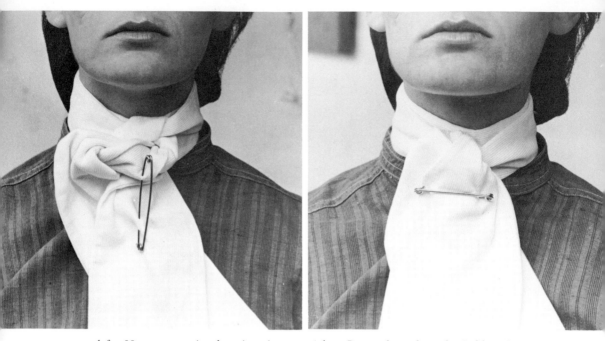

left   How not to tie a hunting tie.   *right*   Correctly and neatly tied hunting tie.

CHILDREN'S SIDESADDLE

Children riding sidesaddle are allowed to wear riding caps. They should not wear veils or, of course, spurs.

9

Training and Schooling

GENERAL TRAINING

To get your horse or pony ready for showing you will need to start in January or February to get the required amount of condition on to stand a hard season in the ring. At whichever show you intend to start – whether Newark or Windsor or just a few local ones – you must start preparing early, gradually increasing your animal's work and feed accordingly. If you follow this rule, it will have a good covering of flesh on its neck and hindquarters. What must be avoided is a gross condition in which your animal is loaded on its shoulders and lumpy round its tail as a result of over-feeding. Animals often appear at shows in youngstock classes like this, and their owners wonder why they go wrong in their feet and wind. At the end of a season, however, all youngstock show horses should be let right down in condition and allowed to run free for

Five-year-old Celtic Gold in his rough state in February. Celtic Gold is a 16.2 hh chestnut gelding, bred in Ireland by Terrence.

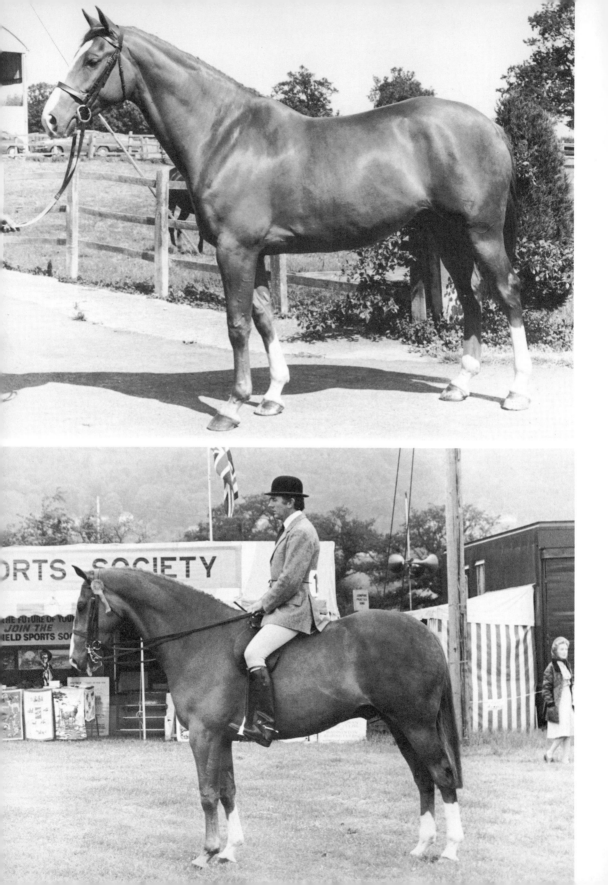

several months until Christmas, after which you can start afresh. This helps to stop them getting excessively fat, which of course is undesirable.

Training and schooling for the show ring should always be done gradually over a period of time. If schooling is rushed before a horse is mentally and physically fit, you may well have problems to correct later. As all showing classes are carried out on the right-hand rein, it is very easy to end up with your animals one-sided and hanging to the centre of the ring. This particularly applies to young animals shown in small rings. It is a great mistake to start schooling for the ring too soon after breaking as the first thing they must be taught is to go forward and be ready to meet the sights and sounds of the showground. Young animals need at least two or three months being quietly hacked out. Obviously there are no hard-and-fast rules, and each one has to be treated as an individual according to its conformation merits, temperament and age. This is what makes producing horses and ponies for the show ring difficult and time-consuming.

Young horses and ponies benefit enormously from being taken to one or two small shows to get them used to the atmosphere and the sights before they are actually shown in the ring. Obviously if they have been shown in hand or have had a season's hunting some of the problems will have been overcome. Until you actually arrive at a showground you cannot be sure how an unshown animal will react as often the quietest of horses can light up. With so many distractions at large shows, such as hot-air balloons, helicopter displays etc., it is no wonder that some of the more highly strung animals play up. Unfortunately, one bad experience at the wrong time can leave an animal upset for several shows after.

It serves as a wonderful education for youngsters to take them during the winter and spring to local indoor schools and suchlike places for ridden schooling and elementary showing. Riding Club activities also provide marvellous experience for novices. No amount of trouble should be spared in getting animals ready for the big early shows. If you are not prepared to make the effort, other people certainly are – and you may

Facing page, top Celtic Gold, six weeks later. After correct work and feeding he is now ready to start the season.

Facing page, bottom Celtic Gold at the Three Counties Show in June of the same year, having been first and reserve champion to Elite. Three days later he was Champion Hunter at the Royal International Horse Show. This picture also shows the rider correctly turned out in ratcatcher attire, suitable for showing in hunter classes.

even get beaten by an inferior animal that is well produced and going confidently for its rider. This particularly applies to four-year-old animals.

Ridden show horses and ponies benefit from hacking out on roads and tracks during the season as this gives them the opportunity to see lots of different sights and sounds and keeps them fresh in themselves as well as maintaining their fitness and muscle. My own horses are ridden out for about one to one and a half hours every day in snaffle bridles and martingales as the latter give extra control in emergencies, such as when a dog runs out. You must take great care when hacking never to let your animal turn round in the road if it sees something it does not like or is suspicious of. If it gets into this habit, it will be difficult to cure and is very likely to behave similarly in the show ring.

Trotting or cantering on grass verges and down lanes, jumping the odd ditch, not only keeps an animal's interest but also helps to balance it naturally. If there are any banks near you which you can walk and trot up and down, so much the better. Just because an animal is a show specimen or has won a few prizes doesn't mean you should wrap it in cotton wool as some people tend to do. Provided that care is taken and you do nothing stupid, no harm should come to it. On road exercise all my animals wear tendon boots in front and knee caps as a protection against knocks or slip-ups.

Too much indoor work can cause a horse to lose his presence and quickly turn sour. This is especially true of older animals. The art of producing show horses is to develop in them a basic natural balance which will encourage a correct, still head carriage which in turn should bring out the best possible movement. In ridden classes it is a combination of horse and rider together – the overall picture – that counts. No show horse should ever have too much right-handed work as he has plenty of that when in the ring. Consequently his ride and way of going will deteriorate if care is not taken with this point. A horse or pony should not be overshown as this will only lead to loss of movement and natural balance and he will probably also become either sour or hot and excitable. The professionals say that three seasons at the top is a horse's usual run of success, though again there will always be exceptions to the rule.

Show animals have to be as well schooled for the top shows as they would for any other equestrian activity. Remember, too, that all the time they are being shown they are in the company of other animals, some cavorting and jumping about in all directions, some sitting on their hind quarters, and others ridden by inconsiderate exhibitors who are quite ignorant and often, unfortunately, without proper control of their mounts.

Youngsters have other factors to contend with as well. Those that are

Hacking in the countryside is a worthwhile part of any horse's training. (This photograph was taken in 1980, before the hard hat controversy had begun. The author now recommends that a hard hat should be worn at all times when riding.)

ridden by judges have to be taught to carry and obey some who are excellent, some middling and some whose knowledge and ability leave a lot to be desired. As one old exhibitor said to me, 'Some would be better and safer inside than on top.' Some judges have lovely sympathetic hands, others are ham-fisted. The same applies to their aids, as all judges are different. You must remember that your horse may go quietly and well for you at home but it is another matter for him to carry a strange judge – and it is often the ride he gives the judge that matters. That being so, it is always wise to get him ridden on one or more occasions prior to his first show by someone at home who has not previously ridden him. This advice is particularly relevant for lightweight lady owners whose mounts are more likely to react badly if a large male judge rides them and they are not used to being ridden by a man at all. Your horse might also have to contend with a judge with long coat tails, so ride him before the show in an old mackintosh to accustom him to the sensation.

If its behaviour is not good, the best-looking exhibit will only go down the line. Manners are essential in all show animals, particularly children's ponies and hacks, and any attempt to nap, hang towards the collecting ring or other horses, or a refusal to stand still either to be mounted or otherwise, are serious faults. Animals that are top-class always appear to flow in their movement and ride, carry the judges well and behave in an exemplary way. Good manners should, of course, always be taught at home, from the moment you walk in to feed your horse or pony in the morning until last thing at night when you look to see if he is comfortable. A well-disciplined animal is always a happy animal. It is when horses are allowed to get away with misbehaviour and bad stable manners that a lot of problems begin.

When horses and ponies have been shown ridden a number of times in the ring, their behaviour often changes, some becoming better, others worse, as they anticipate movements and show-ring procedure. Instinctively they will be waiting for the canter and gallop. They will also find out that when they come to the end of the ring they then have to go down again. This, of course, is when some will try to cut the corners and nap. If allowed to get away with it, they will grow worse at every show, so you must never let them acquire the habit. Always ride exhibits into the corners of the ring if possible and follow the rails by using your inside leg together, if necessary, with your spur to keep them to the outside. You should never pull their heads to the outside, as is often seen, allowing them to swing their quarters out, thus making their whole shape the opposite of what it should be. Once they are allowed to go in this manner it is nearly impossible to cure them, particularly with show hunters that will get stronger and anticipate the gallop.

Be sure that your horse knows how to rein back correctly as he will be required to perform this movement as part of the individual display. To teach a horse or pony to rein back is basic horsemanship. Initially it should be taught from the ground, and in no way should an issue be made of it. Spend a set period on it each day at first. With the help of an assistant it can be taught in long reins, going backwards a step at a time, but the animal should never be allowed to run back. After a few steps back, always make the horse or pony stand and then walk forward again.

When mounted the horse must first stand square and his head must be correctly placed because he will not back with his head in the air. When he is in the correct position, apply pressure with your legs and gently with the reins. As soon as he responds, be satisfied with one or two steps at a time. A rein back should always consist of a series of steps executed with ease and precision. On no account should force be exerted on the mouth as this will only lead to evasion and possibly rearing. At first you can, if you wish, use an assistant to stand in front and help by pressing the horse's chest until he steps back. You can also encourage the animal verbally by saying, 'Back, back'. Reining back is an exercise most animals find difficult to perform and it requires patience from the rider to teach it correctly. Never try to teach reining back with a fresh horse: it is always best done after exercise so that you have the animal's attention.

Training for In-hand Classes

Showing youngstock in hand requires patience and skill to obtain the highest possible placings. We have all seen animals at shows that clearly have been dragged there straight from the field with no proper care or schooling. Youngsters should obviously be taught to be tied up at home in their boxes and to load and unload from transport without any fuss, because if they will not load easily at home there is no way that they will box at a show with all the excitement round them.

Having selected a suitable bridle for your animal, you must teach it to lead correctly by coming up level to your shoulder with its own shoulder. A horse or pony which hangs back looks as bad as one that is pulling to get in front of you. Teach your animal to walk on freely and not to jog. To trot back in hand without any assistance is most essential and something that cannot be over-taught at home. When schooling for this, you really need an assistant to keep the animal up to you and to make it trot back again.

To get an idea of how your animal will behave away from home, it is a good idea to take it to be schooled at a neighbour's house or farm before its first show. A very important point to remember with horses and ponies alike is that they can and do get very attached to one another and, when separated to go to shows or even just into the ring, can become very upset and sometimes impossible to handle. Besides neighing continually they may barge about, a fault which usually results from their being turned out with companions. If this occurs, it is wise to stable them in future as far apart as possible and not turn them out together again during the show season.

It is surprising how many animals will not stand still, even in hand. Much time and trouble must be taken at home to instil this discipline into them. Two- and three-year-olds should always be mouthed and lunged and, if possible, long-reined as this makes them so much easier to handle when away from home. It also prevents a fault seen in so many in-hand show animals: a one-sided mouth. To guard against this further, insist that they are led on the off side as much as possible when at home. It helps to school them in side reins, too, as this stops them cutting in front of you and swinging about.

Lungeing is particularly beneficial to a horse's schooling, if correctly carried out.

Long-reining is an art in itself and should only be attempted by a skilled person.

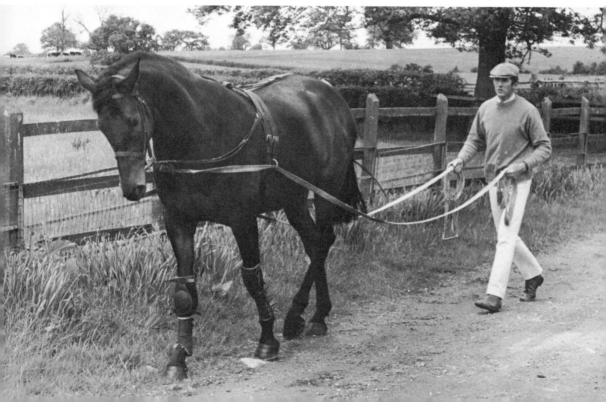

TRAINING FOR A FUTURE CAREER

There comes a time when show animals or potential show animals must start hunting and jumping. And there is no earthly reason why they should not. Correctly made horses and ponies usually jump naturally if taught in the right way from the beginning. However, they still need plenty of care taken of them and their schooling as they are easily over-faced.

To the claim that show animals might get hurt jumping, I always reply that they can just as easily get kicked at a show or fall down on the road. It is most essential that they are taught to jump at home before they go hunting: the hunting field is not the place to teach any animal initially. As regards the ultimate career, be guided by the horse or pony itself.

Remember that it is no good trying to teach your animal to jump in the middle of the show season on rock-hard ground. Ideally the time to teach it is during autumn and winter, then if by any chance it does get a knock it will have time to repair before the season starts. It is also most important, if hunting show animals, to finish the season early. I personally never hunt show horses after 1st February, which allows them time to be prepared for the coming season; if fit and muscled up, they will take time to let down and carry the necessary amount of flesh. I try to cub hunt and go gate shutting with young hunters. This teaches them manners and gives them an interest, especially after a season in the ring. It can also freshen up an older horse. You cannot expect animals to do a full season in the ring and then a full season's hunting, however. Some people do this and wonder why they have no horse left!

On the other hand, if you have a sharp, gassy horse, hunting may well make him worse, particularly if you do not take the trouble to cub hunt him carefully. Ideally, as with all horses, if twice a week he can be hacked to the meet, hunted an hour or two, then hacked home it will be the making of him. If, however, you unbox him at the meet, the excitement of all the other horses together with the sight of the hounds could soon make him unmanageable and stupid. Once he has been introduced to hounds incorrectly, matters can very rarely be put right. Some people go to the opening meet, gallop the guts out of their horse and then wonder why he has no manners and fails to settle to the job. It never ceases to amaze me how some horses are quiet to show under all circumstances and yet quite unmanageable with hounds, and vice versa.

Several years ago I had a lovely novice middleweight that won several leading shows and was as quiet as a lamb to show but when cub-hunted went really silly. One morning when cubbing with my groom, Harry Powell, the horse shook its head, gave a couple of plunges and jumped

straight into the River Wye, a famous salmon river near Hereford. Hounds were drawing a covert on the river fields at the time but fortunately both horse and rider escaped unhurt. He did in fact settle after his ducking although I do not recommend that anyone else tries it.

I like to hunt all my horses as they eventually have to do another job in life and they are prepared if they have been taught to hunt and jump. Horses I have had through my yard have successfully gone on to win races and events, mainly because they were good sorts and were treated with common sense. Show hacks, however, are generally the exception to the hunting rule, being thoroughbred and often highly strung. If they are not taught to hunt and jump with extreme care, they tend to get excited and reach and pull, which in a show hack is the last thing you want.

Hunting can be useful to certain types of horses in furthering their all-round education. This picture shows the author riding the 1980 Champion Show Hunter of the Year, Mrs R. Healey-Fenton's Brigadier; on the right is the late Nimrod Champion, huntsman of the Ledbury foxhounds. This photograph was taken just three weeks after Brigadier had won his Wembley title.

10

Showground Requirements and Travelling

VACCINATION CERTIFICATES

No horse or pony will be admitted to a showground unless it has a current vaccination certificate as laid down by the FEI. The rules state that:

'All horses must have a vaccination certificate completed, signed and stamped by a veterinary surgeon who is not the owner of the animal, stating that it has received a basic primary vaccination against equine influenza. This consists of two injections given not less than twenty-one days and not more than ninety-two days apart. In addition a booster injection must be recorded as having been given within each succeeding twelve months. None of these injections must have been given within the preceding twelve days, including the days of the competition, on entry into the competition stables. This certificate must accompany the horse to all competitions and the competitor is responsible for producing it on demand.'

Be sure to have the dates of the certificate exactly right before you go to a show as if you are out by only one day the officials are quite within their rights to refuse you admission.

Always have your vaccination certificate, height certificate, passports (for thoroughbred stock) and any other relevant documents with you in a folder or box, as I can assure you that many tears and arguments are caused every season, at shows up and down the country, by documents not being produced or in correct order. A typical example was seen at the Royal International Horse Show in 1984, where a hundred horses and ponies were refused admission because their vaccination records did not conform to the FEI requirements. More attention to detail would have avoided this.

Dope Restrictions

Under the rules of shows run by the various official societies no horse or pony can be shown with 'Bute' (Phenylbutazone), tranquillisers or any anti-inflammatory substances in its blood. Persons found guilty of administering any undesirable substances, plus the animals concerned, will be suspended from competition for a period of time decided by the relevant society. If the animal has had veterinary attendance any drug treatment must be out of its system by the time it is shown. Show organisers and the associations reserve the right to carry out random tests and these are performed in accordance with the standard operating procedure prescribed by the veterinary rules of the FEI (International Equestrian Federation). A refusal to submit a horse or pony for the taking of a sample of either blood or urine for analysis is considered a breach of the rules and an owner so doing will have to face the consequences.

Substitution of Entries

None of the various societies will allow substitution of entries at shows. This means that at the early shows where stabling has often to be booked as well as expensive entry fees paid, one has to enter with care and thought, otherwise if for any reason the horse is not shown it becomes very expensive. This is a rule which many exhibitors think could be changed.

First Aid

Both at home and while away at shows it is essential that you have a first-aid box. In the event of an emergency it is important that you have sufficient materials at hand to cope until veterinary help arrives. The following items should prove helpful:

    cotton wool
    gamgee tissue
    gauze
    Animalintex (can be used hot or cold)
    Melolin (a non-adherent, dry, absorbent dressing which I find most useful for cuts etc.; obtainable from chemists or your vet)
    Epsom salts
    salt
    sodium bicarbonate
    colic drench
    Milk of Magnesia

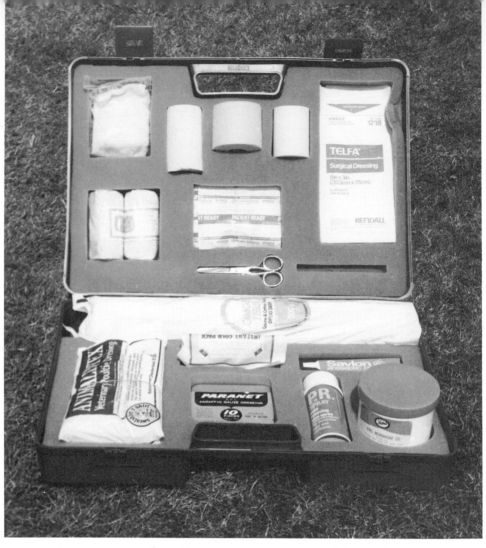

This purpose-made first-aid kit box contains many useful items for coping with an emergency.

      witch hazel lotion
      sulphonamide powder (for wounds etc.)
      antiseptic cream
      Elastoplast bandages (two rolls of 4-inch-wide tape)
      crêpe bandages (various sizes, 2–6 inches wide)
      sharp surgical scissors (kept specifically for first-aid purposes)
      tweezers

It is also advisable to take with you a small first-aid kit for yourself.

    On the market at the moment are various ready-made first-aid kits packed in convenient boxes and containers; many owners find these excellent especially for taking to shows. It is surprising how easily accidents can happen, not only when travelling but also when loading and unloading, and particularly with youngstock, so keep the kit with you wherever you go.

Travelling

When transporting valuable show animals, it is always advisable to have proper travelling equipment to make them as safe and comfortable as possible. Make-do bits and pieces usually fall off on a long journey. It is amazing how a horse or pony can knock himself about while in transit either by slipping or becoming frightened.

First you should fit him with a strong headcollar and provide some form of leg protection. It is now possible to buy manufactured leg guards of various types, but, apart from the fact that they cannot be put on as quickly, leg bandages are just as good if used with either foam pads or, better still, gamgee tissue. The edges of the gamgee tissue can be stitched and it will then last a considerable time.

A tail bandage should be fixed with a tail guard as it is very important that your animal does not arrive with a rubbed tail. On more than one occasion I have witnessed animals arriving at a showground with their tails rubbed red raw through having no protection.

The hocks are the next most important part of the animal to protect: if your trailer or box does not have rubber or matting behind, care must be taken not to allow the hocks to become capped. Hock boots need to be fitted carefully as some young animals object to wearing them, especially the strap-on sort. It is now possible to have foam and plastic ones made that come up above the hock, and these are to be recommended. Your horse or pony should also have a sheet or day rug to wear, depending on the weather. A roller of lightweight type can be fitted to hold the rug and tail-guard in place.

Lastly, for safety in loading and unloading, fit your horse with a pair of knee caps, the top strap of which should be done up tight and the lower one loosely fitted. If by any chance he is travelling by sea or air, a poll-guard and overreach boots all round will give added protection.

Always allow plenty of time for the journey to a show. Nothing makes horses and ponies worse travellers than speed, especially at the start of a journey, because they need a while to find their legs and settle down. Some animals refuse to travel in a tight partition and will lean on the sides. A few will even lie down, which can be frightening. Great care should be taken to give them enough room, and a few short, quiet trips should instil confidence.

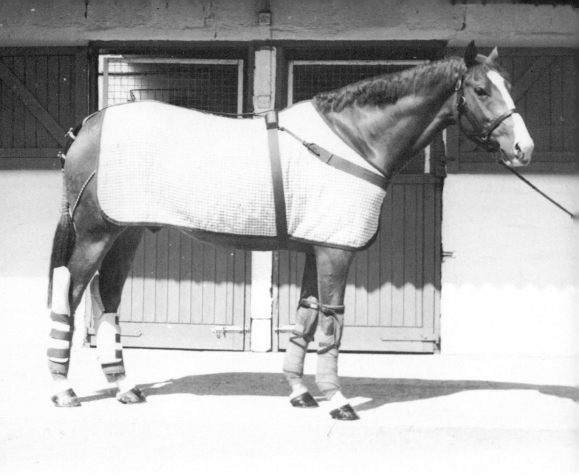

Suitably dressed for summer travelling. This animal has all the necessary protection to prevent an injury during transit.

Only by trial and error will you be able to tell how much clothing your horse will stand while travelling. Some can take one or two rugs, but others need only a sheet otherwise they will sweat up and therefore travel badly. Your time of arrival should be decided the night before the show and will depend on whether you have a novice, a horse or pony that needs a certain amount of riding in, or one that can be shown straight from the lorry. On arriving at the gate of the showground, have all the necessary passes and documents ready to hand over to the person in charge. This again can save time and trouble.

SHOWGROUND PRECAUTIONS

Because horses and ponies are often put into temporary wooden boxes at shows and can easily injure themselves by kicking through the thin boards of which these boxes are made, it is advisable to leave stable bandages on

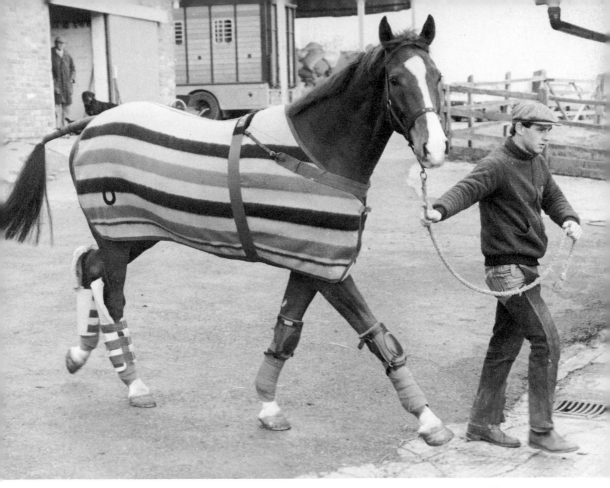

Another example of a horse correctly protected for travelling. This particular animal has just arrived from Ireland and is wearing a warm woollen day rug.

wherever possible, as a prevention against cuts and knocks. Before putting your animal into any temporary stabling check the box for protruding nails etc. which could cause trouble.

When staying away at shows remember to take extra rugs with you because most portable stables are poorly insulated and much colder than your stables at home. I always put an extra blanket on my horses when they are stabled in temporary boxes as I know they will feel the cold if I don't. Often, if the weather is wet, I put a New Zealand rug on top of the horse's normal stable clothing as I feel this gives added protection.

Another item which I take to shows is a portable grille for the top doors of the boxes – this saves any fighting with the horse or pony next door.

You are also advised to take a portable manger as very few shows now put them in. It is most essential you take your own feed and hay with you as well. Although some shows do sell it it may well not be of the same quality that your horse is used to at home. Moreover a change of food might well put your exhibit off its feed, which is the last thing you want.

Although some shows do provide bedding it is often sparse and sometimes inferior. It is therefore wise to take your own, especially if you bed your horse on shavings. A sudden change to inferior straw, which your animal may well eat, could leave your horse with a cough or colic.

11

Show-Ring Procedure and Ringcraft

Arrival at a Show

On arrival at a show, large or small, it is always in the interests of all concerned to have a set plan. If you stick as near as possible to that plan, you will always be on time and organised.

Time is of the utmost importance. You must always be alert for announcements of any time changes during a show to ensure punctuality. I have seen exhibitors missing not only classes but championships and prizegivings too. There is no possible excuse for not paying attention. You must also always remember that stewards and officials are only doing their duty and are not paid professionals. Arguments only get you and the show a bad name.

It is beneficial in the case of youngsters and even some older animals to let them graze after a journey. This can help them to settle down better than if you started riding or lungeing them straight away. Again, though, there cannot be any hard-and-fast rules: every exhibit is different. Remember that your aim is to have a settled, quiet animal to show, which of course is what the judge will be looking for.

If you arrive at a show where the ground is hard, providing the animal has been well schooled at home it should be sufficient just to ride the horse at walk for between thirty minutes to an hour before entering the ring, to acquaint the animal with the sights and sounds of the show ground. In all probability this will do more good, both mentally and physically, than a lot of wild cantering about, but you must always ride the horse right up to the bridle and not allow it to slop about aimlessly. The horse must also be made to face everything it sees and never permitted to turn away from something it dislikes as this easily leads to nappiness and disobedience. If you allow your horse to get away with this sort of behaviour it can be very difficult to eradicate – and unfortunately this is evident in a lot of show ponies today.

Do not make the mistake of giving your animal so much work before a competition that it loses any presence it may have had, is flat and lifeless when in the ring and gives the judges a dull ride.

Send someone to collect your number from the secretary's tent and check the location of your show ring and the route to it, because if you leave this to the last minute there can be confusion. If you are competing in a ridden class, check that your saddle and bridle are fitted correctly. Time and trouble should not be spared in this: it is attention to detail that makes all the difference between winning and losing. Make sure that your keepers are in safe on the bridle and everything adjusted correctly. Then quietly walk your animal in by walking and trotting about the showground. Remember that animals will usually light up when in the ring in the company of others, while being perfectly well behaved outside. If a friend or groom is with you, he or she can tidy up the animal ready for the class after you have worked it, while you yourself get changed into your show clothes.

FINAL TOUCHES

Before entering the show ring it is essential to put the final touches to your animal by giving a final wipe with the stable rubber to remove any dust. The tack should be given one last wipe with a sponge of saddle soap. The animal's eyes and nose can have a little baby oil applied to take away the dry look of the skin in summer or, if preferred, Vaseline can be used. One of the proprietary brands of hoof oil can be applied to the feet. If your horse or pony has a white sock or leg - which will, of course, have been washed - you can, if you wish, apply some chalk whitening. The whole picture should now look spotless.

In hack and riding show-pony classes it is customary to put squares or patterns on the quarters using an ordinary hair comb cut to whatever size you think suits your animal best. First, dampen the quarters with a sponge or water brush and, starting at the top, draw down one comb's square, then leave a comb's width, and so on until you have a draught-board appearance. With practice at home it can be done in quite a short time and looks very attractive when well executed. Lower down the quarters, many people apply what are termed shark's teeth. These are put on with a damp body brush from a standing position behind the animal and involve 'drawing' a series of straight lines towards you across the horse's quarters, then making sloping vertical strokes, half crossing each line in turn, so that the desired shape is produced.

When ready you can make your way to the collecting ring in plenty of time before the class is due in the show ring. And as they say in Ireland, 'Go away and enjoy yerself as you are now in d'hands of d'man in d'middle.' The more relaxed you are, the better your animal will perform.

RIDDEN CLASSES

Into the ring

When the exhibit and rider are ready to enter the ring, both should be as calm and collected as possible. Any nervousness on the part of the rider will be immediately transmitted to the horse. Most riding classes follow the same procedure. When the signal is given by the steward for exhibits to enter the ring, there is no order of precedence. It is always wise to walk in rather than trot or canter. The most important thing is to keep well away from other exhibits and avoid bunching, a particular fault of children who tend to get on top of each other make judging difficult. Keeping space between exhibits enables judges to see more clearly what they have in front of them. Ride your horse well up into his bridle and let him walk on. Never overtake in front of the judges if at all possible as this is considered very bad etiquette by all and sundry. Unfortunately, some exhibitors think it is a clever move, usually children trying to impress the judge.

The walk may be done in a small area of the ring. When asked to trot on, you should take up a wider area to allow yourself room. If bunching is likely, do a small circle into more space. The art of show-ring riding is to have space at all times which will allow your exhibit to settle more, as well as giving the judges the chance to see you properly. When in the ring many judges will look behind them so as well as watching the steward, who is giving the orders of the class, you should keep an eye on the judge.

In the trot it is essential to keep your horse balanced and not to move too fast, another very bad fault often seen in show-pony classes. Using as much of the ring as possible, maintain a level slow trot, particularly when passing the judge. When asked to canter on, do not be in a hurry. This is the pace that should enable you to get into position for the gallop required in hunter and cob classes. You should not allow any anticipation in your animal: hunters and cobs should canter covering the ground, whereas ponies and hacks should canter very collectedly and slower.

When showing a hunter or cob, canter round the ring several times, remembering to go into all the corners. As the order is given to gallop, gradually glide into it past the judge in single file if possible. Do not over-gallop, gallop round corners or overtake unnecessarily. If you do any of these, particularly with high-couraged youngsters, after one or two shows they will start to pull and rush together, usually throwing their heads about in an unsightly manner. Gallop down one side of the ring only, not round and round as if it were a racetrack. It is advisable to use

A line-up of cobs at Royal Windsor.

your voice when going into a corner to steady your mount, but not so that the entire showground can hear you. You should also use light aids to bring your animal back into control in a well-mannered way.

After the order to walk again has been given, trot briskly to the centre. It is now vital to have all your wits about you so as not to get missed in the walk round or hidden behind jumps. If you give your horse a pat on the neck at this stage and ride on a longer rein, he should settle back down and walk out. All exhibits will now be lined up either to give an individual show or be ridden or, in the case of hacks and riding horses, both.

In individual shows of hacks and riding horses, hacks are never asked to gallop either together or singly. The length of the show should not exceed one and a half minutes and should include walk, trot, canter on, both reins, canter out (extended canter), rein back, and a good, obedient halt. In all hack classes there is strong emphasis on manners. Novice hacks

Line-up of small hacks at Stoneleigh, prior to giving their individual shows.

should not be asked too much of in individual shows; the wise exhibitor will just give a short, well-balanced display. The judge will be looking for a show as smooth and uncomplicated as possible with no resistance and little or no anticipation in the animal. Long, repetitive shows only cause judges to walk away and call for the next exhibit.

The judge's ride

When it comes to your turn for the judge to ride your exhibit, have it standing squarely on all four legs and looking alert, and if possible have the stirrup leathers adjusted to approximately the right length. The steward will nearly always give the judge a leg-up for you, although some judges may prefer to use the stirrup and get on themselves. I always do this when judging hacks as in my opinion it is a good test of manners if they stand still. In training your show animal, make a point of insisting it stands still not only while you are mounting but afterwards until it is given the aid to move off. Failure to teach it this will at times lose you a class or lower your placing. Do not get into conversation with the judge but be as polite and helpful as you can and when he brings your exhibit back thank him, even if, in your opinion, he has ridden it badly. Remember, you were not asked to show it under him, you took it there for his opinion.

The groom's role in the ring

After the horse has been ridden or, in the case of a pony, given an individual show, the removal of the saddle will be requested, or stripping as it is often referred to. It is at this point that the groom should come in to help. Your groom should be neat and tidy, wearing a jacket, collar and tie and a suitable hat. Many shows now give some quite good prizes for

Line-up of working hunters.

the best turned-out groom – an excellent idea which helps to keep up the standard of turn-out. Unfortunately, some grooms, particularly at the smaller shows, leave a lot to be desired where appearance is concerned, being far from clean and tidy. It is no excuse to say that they have a lot to do prior to coming into the ring; a tidy groom in the ring is most likely to be the one who is conscientious at home with regard to his or her animals' welfare.

Grooms need to bring into the ring firstly a rug or sheet, depending on the weather. If it is cold and wet, your horse or pony could easily catch a chill after he has been galloping unless care is taken. A box or bucket containing a damp sponge, stable rubber, body brush and hoof oil should also be brought. It is advisable to include a hoof pick too in case a stone may have been picked up and cause your animal to pull out lame. Get your groom quickly to wipe over and generally tidy up the exhibit. The time you have to do this will, of course, depend on the number of entries forward.

The in-hand inspection

When asked by the steward to bring your horse out to be inspected for conformation and action in hand, look sharp. You should previously have moved him from a standing position as he may have gone cold: something that should have been well practised at home beforehand. Nothing looks worse than an exhibit dragged out like a dead dog in front of the judge. Get your groom to give the animal a click from behind and possibly a flick with the stable rubber to make him pay attention and be alert. Don't look back at him when you lead him out, but only in the direction you are going, stand him four square and, when asked to walk off sharply, after a given distance turn to your right, pushing the exhibit away from you. When square, trot on sharply and do not stop until well past the judge, keeping in a straight line.

So many people wander about when showing in hand that they can often go down a place to an inferior animal that comes out and gives an excellent in-hand show. It is a good tip, if showing a youngster, to have your groom sited at the point of the turn back to help send the animal on in its trot. This, of course, should be well practised at home beforehand. Remember that you cannot take too much care over impressing the judge. A sloppy, inferior show can put you down; if you perform impressively, up you will come, to everyone's delight.

Bringing a horse forward for conformation judging.

Trotting up a horse in hand.

The judgment

You will be asked to put the saddle back on and walk round in a small circle with the other exhibitors. Keep your animal alert and well together as this is when the judge makes his final assessment of the class. When you are all placed – though often it will just be the first six to eight – the rest will be asked to leave the ring. If you are among the number asked to go, this is a time to show sportsmanship. If your animal has gone badly, or in your own opinion you have been harshly done by, *never* come out of the ring jabbing the poor creature in the mouth or kicking it with your spurs. This only gives showing, especially to outsiders, a bad name. It is your own fault if you have not done sufficient work at home. Take a mental note of what you think you did wrong and try to improve on your next outing.

Final walk round of lightweight hunters at the Royal Show.

If by any chance your horse or pony has misbehaved or hotted up through the excitement, do not start immediately to canter him round in small circles which will only tend to wind him up more. Go back to the horsebox, put on your own working clothes in place of your showing dress and quietly walk your animal about for as long as you think it needs to settle – one to two hours if necessary. Time spent now will pay

Showing is certainly not without its lighter moments. Here three 'nagsmen' – Vin Toulson (left), the author and David Tatlow – enjoy a joke together.

dividends in the future. Just stand it in the collecting ring area or there-abouts and let it take in all the sights and sounds. It is also a very good idea, if time permits, to put the animal away and then get it out again later. Only by taking time and trouble in this way will you succeed with a young or high-couraged animal, *and* you will be saving wear and tear on your horse's joints – an essential precaution in top show exhibits.

IN-HAND CLASSES

Having groomed and settled your exhibit make your way to the collecting ring in plenty of time.

When in the ring it is essential for the handler and the horse to walk on but to keep a good distance from the exhibit in front of you as many youngsters tend to kick. Pay attention to the steward when you are called into position and be ready for your turn to come out in front of the judge. Remember to stand your horse up correctly, keeping his head in the right position, neither too high nor too low (pick a piece of grass to make him interested).

Having closely inspected your animal the judge will ask you to walk your horse away and to trot back. It is most essential that you have practised this part beforehand. When turning to trot back always walk one or two paces before you trot as this allows the animal to balance itself for a good level return. Keep going well beyond the judge, in a straight line. Take a short hold on the bridle reins or lead rein as in doing so you will maintain much more control.

Many in-hand exhibits nibble or bite their handler or try to chew the reins. If your horse should try this, right at the beginning give him a good smack on the nose and stop him immediately. This can be a very bad habit and difficult to eradicate once allowed to develop. Horses must learn to respect their handler at all times. Do not, as one often sees, niggle and jab at in-hand exhibits' mouths as this often leads to problems later in life when the horses are ridden.

There is much more to successfully showing in-hand than people imagine but if time and trouble is taken the end results can be very successful and rewarding.

Children's Classes

In all classes children have to learn ringcraft, as no matter how good their pony is they will not have much success if not taught this art. Some children are experts from an early age, while others have to learn to improve as they go along, there being no substitute for experience. Presenting the pony to the judge is, in fact, very much a matter of commonsense. Children should be taught to make full use of the ring and not to crowd.

The trot is a pace that needs to be taken carefully; far too many children trot too fast with their ponies' hocks trailing along behind. When asked to canter on, they should wait until reaching a corner, which will help the pony to strike off on the required leg. This rule applies particularly to novice children and ponies.

After the individual show, which should be as simple and correct as possible, encouraging the child to use as much space as is available in front of the judge, you then come to the in-hand phase. This is where ponies can easily go up or down, depending on the quality of presentation. No amount of practice at home is wasted. It is essential that the pony comes out easily and level with the child and stands square to be assessed. When the exhibit walks away, make sure it turns right-handed and trots back in a straight line, continuing well beyond the judge. Children should be encouraged to watch either older children or competitors in adult classes when professionals are showing. Parents must remember that showing should be enjoyable to the child and pony and can help teach good manners and sportsmanship.

12

Hunters

The showing of hunters, particularly English-Irish bred hunters, has always had a fascination for people from many walks of life and different parts of the world. We also have the breeders, trainers and riders to compete on them successfully. The bigger, thoroughbred horse of 'chasing type which people used to breed out of some of the loveliest old mares, not only to race but also to show, hunt and event, are growing fewer and fewer. On the racecourse there are much smaller animals now 'chasing and hurdling than there used to be. The constant emphasis on speed has ensured that they are bred smaller.

One of the finest types of hunter is the light-middleweight that is thoroughbred. If you are clever enough to breed one of these, you are very lucky indeed, because they have the stamina and quality to gallop and jump all day. From the show ring, champions have been found to go racing, eventing and show jumping. It is a great shop window from which horses are bought to go all over the world. To compete in the show ring is obviously a great schooling ground in every sense for both horse and rider.

For future competition work people are today trying to breed hunters from small mares crossed with the Irish draught stallion, the aim being to have more bone and weight. This seems to be working well as there are so many mares lacking bone and size that, if they are put back to thoroughbred, the progeny are small animals suitable only for ladies and teenagers. Another cross which seems to work well is that of the Welsh cob stallion crossed on thoroughbred and hunter mares. The stock seem to have very fine temperaments and are good, active rides.

With their mild climate and limestone soil, the Irish still seem able to breed the quality middleweight to heavyweight horse that so many people envy and need. Crossing the traditional Irish draught mare with the thoroughbred horse is how the best animals were and still are bred. The best Irish draught mares are always good movers and have very little or no hair in their heels. Many people do not realise that they stand only 15.2 to 16 hh, which just goes to show you do not need height to breed bone and size. The ideal brood mare is always a good type but must be free of unsoundness, such as bad feet, side bone, ringbones or curbs, all of which are easily passed on to their progeny.

We are now seeing in the show ring youngstock of Dutch-German blood. These animals have good-shaped forelegs and size, and are usually good movers and can often extend in their trot. Unfortunately, the ones which have been ridden do appear rather long in the back, and often have a high tail carriage which looks unattractive. In the next year or two, however, we will observe many more of these and we will then be able to give a better opinion of them. They are, of course, popular with the show-jumping and dressage fraternity but I doubt if the eventing and hunting people will agree with them. Many say that they cannot gallop and stay. It is quite probable that the mares of this foreign cross, when mated to our thoroughbred horses, could easily breed what we are looking for. Some foreign breeds have small, boxy feet, which many breeders are trying to eradicate. They have successfully got rid of curby hocks, however, a fault which is still seen in our British horses.

The show hunter should be as near perfect a model in its class as possible. It should have imposing presence and courage. It always used to be said that 'A good big 'un will always beat a good little 'un,' which still seems the rule today, as on only rare occasions will a small hunter ever be made champion over the weighted classes. This only usually happens at small, one-day shows, and could be because the value of small hunters does not compare with that of the large ones. But I have seen some faultless small hunters which are unfortunately not eligible to go forward in major championships.

The show hunter's movement is always a very controversial subject. Everyone agrees that they should move straight, because if the feet turn in or out, or there is any sign of dishing, there will be strain on the legs and tendons which can lead to all sorts of troubles. Whether or not you want daisy-cutting action is up to you. Very few extravagant movers ever really jump well. There is a school of thought – one to which I myself subscribe – that hates to see a hunter put its heel down on the ground first so that you sometimes glimpse the sole of its foot. Movement is a subject that nobody will agree on.

The dressage and show-jumping people are also looking for something different: the daisy cutter is certainly out of favour with them. I personally like to see a horse that is natural and loose in its movement, one which is able to lengthen and shorten its stride and has as little knee action as possible but also uses its shoulders. I like to see a good hunter really walk out. The racing fraternity say that if a horse can really walk and put his toe out, he can always gallop. It is a waste of time showing a horse that is not a good mover as, nine times out of ten, he will be beaten by an animal of possibly not as good conformation but which moves well.

At the leading shows, classes for hunters are made up as follows:

Four-year-old Hunters of any Height or Weight

This is always a most interesting class in that it brings out horses which were shown in three-year-old classes the previous season. Many champion hunters for one reason or another fail to make the grade when ridden, and young potential swans are seen to become ducks. Often they appear short in front and unable to gallop, and as a result of being shown in hand they lose their natural presence as they have seen it all too often in their led days.

In recent years one outstanding young animal which did live up to its early promise was the chestnut gelding Royal Fiddler which I showed for his breeder. Fiddler has the distinction of being Champion Young Hunter at the Royal Show when only a yearling. Consequently he was a champion at many leading shows as a two- and three-year-old, qualifying for the Lloyds Bank In-hand Championship every year. When produced as a four-year-old, among other shows he won the Royal and the Royal International. He was a very good mover and a comfortable ride, but from his in-hand days he did not have the best of mouths.

Often people will not show in youngstock classes as they believe that their animals should be running free and natural all summer and not be treated as hot-house plants that melt away and die when ridden. Four-year-old hunters must be riding well to have any chance at the leading shows. Ideally they should have seen hounds if possible and been out in company with lots of other horses or be very advanced in their schooling.

One point to note as regards showing a four-year-old is not to over-gallop it in the ring. This very quickly leads to anticipation on the horse's part and tends to make it pull and reach at you. As you can well imagine, ten to twenty four-year-olds galloping together are bound to hot up.

Because four-year-olds come in every shape and size, it is possible for a winning four-year-old to grow by the following season into a horse that is between his weights or 'not a correct weight', i.e. not big enough to be classed as a middleweight but too big to be a lightweight. However, he can always compete in working-hunter or ladies' classes and, of course, at shows with open and only two weight divisions. If you only show your four-year-old in four-year-old classes, he is eligible to compete in novice classes the next season. The wise owner of a good four-year-old will show him sparingly and then enter him in a few novice classes as a five-year-old. By showing him hounds and teaching him to jump in the autumn you should then, if all goes well, have a good horse to show when he is six years old. Some owners of good three-year-olds never show them as four-year-olds but prefer to keep them until they are five years old and bring them out as novices.

It is difficult to show a horse as a four-year-old as obviously he is still immature both physically and mentally. He often appears fresh when in company, but when given sufficient work to make him behave he tires quickly and loses his natural way of going. It is also easy to jar up and sour a four-year-old by too much work on hard going at shows. He does need to be fit and well but to show him in the ring fresh is of no use to you, the judge or the horse himself. In the case of an animal of this age, you have to discover by trial and error how best to produce him for the ring. Some require a great deal of work while others will manage on a little. The way they are brought on is of great importance, for if they are always made to behave from the start at home, with any luck they should behave at a show. I never allow any of my horses to buck or mess about without severely reprimanding them, because if they are allowed to get away with it, they will surely let you down in public, when good behaviour matters most.

Four-year-olds can, if you like, be shown in a snaffle bridle, and obviously if you feel that your horse goes sufficiently well in one and you can hold him while galloping with other horses, do so.

WEIGHT CLASSES

One of the most controversial subjects in the showing of hunters is that of weights. The three weight classes are lightweight (that is, not to carry more than 12 stone 7lb), middleweight (12 stone 7lb to 14 stone) and heavyweight (14 stone and over). People have and always will argue about a particular horse's weight, because it is not height that carries weight but the bone below the knee. This is measured with a tape measure just under the knee. Approximate guide measurements are: lightweight $8\frac{1}{2}$ inches; middleweight, $8\frac{1}{2}$ to 9 inches; and heavyweight 9 inches and over. There always has to be a top and bottom weight in a class and, of course, it is these that are the problem. Although they may appear wrong in one class, they also often look out of place in the next, perhaps being too large for one and too small for the next. These horses are often referred to as 'having no showing weight' and 'not having a true weight class'. The stamp of horse also makes a difference as a tall, narrow animal often appears up to more weight than it actually is. This type rarely does well in the show ring and often does not stand work in other types of competition. It is the nice, short-legged horse which is the workman, deep of its body and with a good, sloping shoulder, short-backed and with a fair set of limbs, having an attractive outlook and lots of natural presence.

Lightweights

The lightweight classes at the major shows are usually the best filled and often contain some really high-class horses. Lightweights are usually easier to breed and buy, many being thoroughbreds or seven-eighths. The ideal horse for this class is 16.1–16.2 hh with about $8\frac{1}{2}$ inches of bone below the knee. The lightweight horse must be a good mover and be able to gallop and, as this is a strong class to win, he must have plenty of presence to stand out among the others. The lightweight needs to be well schooled and light in the hand, and should not pull or lean on the hands as would be more acceptable in the heavyweight horse. Far too many lightweight horses we see in the ring would be much too strong a ride both in size and manners for the average lightweight rider. A true lightweight should be an ideal ride for ladies and lightweight men to ride, hunt or event, but in no way should he be a hack type as is sometimes seen.

Swanborne, Royal International Champion Lightweight Hunter. This 16.1 hh bay gelding has $8\frac{1}{2}$ inches of bone below the knee. A true pattern of lightweight show hunter.

Unfortunately, far too many lightweights shown are above the recognised carrying weight of 12 stone 7lb, and some are even down in the catalogues as being 17 hh. No lightweight should be that high if insufficient bone makes them lightweight. In my opinion, they should be shown as giraffes! Judges confronted with large classes of perhaps twenty horses ranging from 15.3 to 17 hh, all calling themselves lightweight, certainly have a task. When the judges ride the horses they will find that some are narrow, while others are very wide and cobby. However, the truly made lightweight should win the day.

Middleweights

To many people the high-class middleweight is the most admirable. He is possibly the most valuable to own, and in the best hunting countries the middleweight blood horse of up to 14 stone is envied by most people. If by any chance he is thoroughbred of hunter type, he is rare indeed. If good enough, the middleweight horse satisfies most judges' ideal in championships.

Elite, many times champion middleweight, ridden by Vin Toulson.

The ideal pattern for a middleweight is about 16.3 hh with about $8\frac{3}{4}$ to 9 inches of bone below the knee. The middleweight horse has a wider range in its class than either the lightweight or heavyweight. He should ride bold and take hold of his bridle; in fact, he should 'look like a lion and ride like a lamb' as that great showman of the past, Jack Gittens, always told me.

Jack was one of the great past masters of showing hunters and rode no fewer than ten Royal Dublin champions for the late Nat Galway-Grear. Many of them found their way to England to continue their winning ways. Jack showed his horse on a long rein yet always managed to have complete control and balance.

One of my middleweight horses that I shall never forget was the thoroughbred brown gelding Dual Gold by La'du'd'or. He was bought at Doncaster sales as a four-year-old by that great judge of a horse and showman, Vin Toulson. When shown at five years, he was unbeaten in many outings. As a six-year-old he was bought for me to show by Mr and Mrs Peter White of Sussex. He continued to win for three seasons, being three times Middleweight of the Year at the Horse of the Year

Dual Gold, an exceptional type of thoroughbred middleweight, standing 17 hh with 9 inches of bone.

Dual Gold won the Middleweight of the Year title at Wembley on three consecutive occasions (1977, 1978 and 1979) and was 1980 Working Hunter of the Year. Notice the well-fitting clothes of the rider. Dual Gold is considered by the author to be the best horse he has ridden across country.

Show in London. The following year, ridden by my wife Gillian, he was unbeaten in working hunters and finished as the Working Hunter of the Year. Every year he was hunted well and could jump any type of fence he was required to. I hunted him with many different packs and he would jump the Berkeley rhines as well as the Ledbury gates. A great horse indeed, he measured 17 hh and had 9 inches of bone. He was one of the best rides I shall ever sit on.

Only at the smaller shows is the middleweight sometimes at a disadvantage when only two classes are held and there is indecision as to which division is best for him. Up to 13 stone 7lb and over, one has to decide which for the day he is, either lightweight or heavyweight.

Heavyweights

The true heavyweight show horse capable of carrying over 14 stone is a rare commodity today. So many are not up to weight, and then there are the common, slow, ugly brutes that years ago would be pulling a cart. The blood horse to carry 15 stone is difficult to find and even more difficult to breed. Free movers with good, flat bone – not the round, common bone of the cart horse – are the ones you require. Some common horses are clipped and trimmed to within an inch of their life in the pretence of being show heavyweights, but as soon as they move the story is different.

Mrs Veronica White's Flashman, a sensational heavyweight hunter, bred in Ireland by Wilton House. Winner of Wembley's prestigious Show Hunter of the Year title as well as many other championships. His correct conformation, together with floating action and a wonderful temperament, enabled him to win so much.

The quality heavyweight show horse is the monarch of the ring and the envy of everyone. His trot is not as spectacular as that of the lightweight or middleweight, but it is still long and low with little or no knee action. The true heavyweight need not be more than 17 hh but should have 9 or 10 inches of bone below the knee. Where the blood heavyweight comes into his own is in the gallop. Here he leaves his common brothers floundering behind him. Ireland still seems to be able to produce this type of animal, bred by the thoroughbred out of the old Irish draught-type mare. Indeed, in England, after several lean years we now have a fine selection of show heavyweights, most of them Irish-bred.

The heavyweight does need time to mature and is best not shown until he is six years old when he can stand the rigours of the showground. Unfortunately, as with all big horses, his wind has to be carefully looked after. Get him fit with plenty of quiet road work to start the season, and at any sign of cough or cold lay him off work until he is fit again. Failure to do this will surely render him more likely to make a noise and consequently useless for the show ring. Many people show their heavyweight horses too fat and unfit, which can lead to trouble. There is no doubt that if you are lucky enough to own a good heavyweight, great care must be taken to keep him right and sound.

At the end of the show season it is essential to take the show condition off your heavyweight and let him down quietly. Failure to do so will cause strain on his legs and joints, and he may become loaded with flesh on his shoulders which will be wide to sit on if it is allowed to remain.

SMALL HUNTERS

It gives me great pleasure to write on small hunters as it was the first class with which I had great success at the start of my career. It was with a 15.2 hh brown gelding called Lord Sorcerer by a Hunters Improvement Society stallion called More Magic. Lord Sorcerer won at many of the leading shows in the country for three seasons, including the Horse of the Year Show. He worked very hard too, as every winter he was regularly hunted. He was a great jumper and right to the end of his days had fine, clean limbs. This only goes to show that a horse, if correctly made and looked after, can do a great deal of work.

The true small hunter should be based on the miniature middleweight pattern. He should be short on the leg with a good, deep body and, to use an old term, a 'very butty' type. He should have a lot of character and presence about him to be good. Movement in a small hunter needs to be especially attractive as it is not unusual to have about twenty competing together at any one time. It is a very popular class because any member of the family can ride the horse and manage him, from children just out of pony classes to dear old grandmother. He is, or at least he should be, more easily maintained and managed than his larger counterparts. Originally the small hunter had to be shown by people under the age of twenty-one, but after several years this rule was generally dropped and now only the occasional show insists on it. The small hunter makes an excellent mount for children coming off ponies who do not want to show a hack. He has the added advantage that, with him, you are able to go in for many different branches of equestrianism as well if you wish.

Major and Mrs J. Helme's champion small hunter, Lord Sorcerer, a 15.2 hh brown gelding by More Magic. Lord Sorcerer was the author's first winner at the Horse of the Year Show, in 1970, when he won the Small Hunter of the Year title. Not only was he a champion show horse but he was hunted regularly every season as well. Note correct tack, well-plaited mane and length of tail.

In the show ring at the present time we are seeing many hack/riding-horse-type animals which lack both the limb and body to be true small hunters. These often move very prettily and find favour with a few judges, particularly if very well schooled. Of course, it is possible to have a lot of fun at the smaller shows with this type of animal because it is very versatile and eligible to compete in many different classes.

Judges always seem to differ in their opinion as to what constitutes a top small show horse. At one show a horse will be top and the following week could easily be down the line. If you show small hunters, this is one thing you must learn to accept. There always seems to be controversy on small hunter heights too, many people maintaining that they are over 15.2 hh. A good sort of 15.2 hh appears from the outside of the ring to be higher than it is, and so much depends on the animal's withers being high or low. If you are lucky enough to find a small show hunter mare with bone and substance, after her ridden days are over she will make a really excellent brood mare, capable of breeding larger animals than herself if mated to the right sire.

At the larger shows there are small hunter brood mare classes. Two outstanding recent winners are Mrs Gibson's Gamelyn which was by that wonderful sire of show horses, Game Rights, and Mrs D. Nicholson's Little Primrose which won the Lloyds Bank Championship at the Horse of the Year Show at Wembley.

At shows in some parts of the country, particularly Devon and Cornwall, there are small hunter youngstock classes. In view of the amount of interest in them and the number of small horses bred, it is a great pity that more shows do not put these classes on as they would surely be well supported. The classification is as follows: yearlings should not exceed 14.3 hh, two-year-olds should not exceed 15 hh, and three-year-olds should not exceed 15.1 hh. Occasionally, with only one class in the schedule, the animals are to be under 15.1 hh on the day of the show. Sometimes they are measured on the showground which occasionally leads to arguments if an animal has passed at an earlier show and now fails to measure, perhaps because it is on its toes. As height certificates are not issued, however, one must accept the vet's opinion.

LADIES' SIDESADDLE

It is usually stipulated that ladies' hunter classes are to be ridden sidesaddle. Occasionally they are open to astride only, but in both classes the judge will be looking for the ideal ladies' hunter, not only of correct conformation but also a light, well-balanced ride and forward going. In this class it is possible to find a very good ladies' horse which just misses being

Brewster, a 16.2 hh brown gelding, seen here winning at the Royal International, ridden by Sophie Waddilove. Brewster had a wonderful show-ring career ranging from winning championships in hand to being Lightweight Show Hunter of the Year.

top-class in the weights, usually because of being on the small side. If the owner takes the trouble to school the animal well both astride and side-saddle, however, she can have a lot of fun with it.

In recent years the popularity of ladies' sidesaddle riding has escalated to great heights. Sidesaddle clothes have come to the fore again, many being brought out smelling of mothballs when it was thought there was no further use for them. Moreover, such outfits have risen in value from a few pounds to hundreds. The Sidesaddle Association has done a wonderful job in bringing sidesaddle riding back to the popularity it holds today.

The show hunter class ridden by a lady sidesaddle, which is judged on the horse, should not be confused with equitation classes which are judged on the rider only. Many shows now include the latter class in their schedules. They are called sidesaddle equitation classes and are either open or there are separate classes for adult and junior riders (sixteen years and under). Horses may be ridden in any bridle and must be four years old or over. Marks are awarded for the saddle and the way in which it is fitted. The rider then has to perform a test to show her riding capabilities which consists of a figure of eight, walk, trot and extended canter. The rider is also judged on straightness, suppleness and horsemanship. These are excellent classes to encourage people to show and for people who cannot or do not want to purchase a top show animal. To compete in them riders must be members of the Sidesaddle Association.

Horses and ponies must have a very good front and go forward freely to carry a sidesaddle satisfactorily. Often horses with long backs do the job well. If care is taken gradually to introduce them to it and the saddle fits well, there is no reason why they should object at all. Many horses go well from the first time it is put on. If you have any doubts, however, it is always beneficial to get expert advice.

YOUNG HUNTERS

For many the showing of young hunters is a waste of time and money, often wearing the animals out before their time. Some people also believe that animals shown in hand never go on to greater heights but are rendered good for nothing! But for others the satisfaction of breeding and producing young hunters holds a fascination that nothing else can match. Breeding or producing any prizewinner or, for that matter, the champion at the Hunter Show or the Royal, or even your local agricultural show must give you the utmost satisfaction, especially if it is out of your favourite mare that in all probability was at one time herself a winner in the show ring before carrying you safely during many seasons' hunting.

The judges in hunter breeding classes have perhaps the hardest task of all those who officiate in the show ring. They must not only differentiate between the best animals that are put before them but be capable too of looking into the future and determining what sort of horse the youngster is going to develop into when he matures, for young horses are apt to alter. The big yearling often goes common and the opposite is equally true, for many underbred-looking youngsters grow into quality and fine down almost beyond belief as they mature. It is a matter for considerable speculation that very many of the big winners in hand turn out to be second-rate when they return to the ring under saddle. Some, indeed, are deemed to be not worth showing and fade out of the picture completely when their led days are over. In the case of hunter-bred youngsters, the fact that many grow coarse with advancing years is undoubtedly a contributing cause and one which does not apply to quality young animals that may deteriorate in every other way but at least don't lose their quality. Another equally important factor is that, as far as action is concerned, the led horse can only be judged on his walk and his trot. His galloping potential cannot be put to the test, but a good shoulder freely used, great length from the hips to the hock and a long, easy stride are indicative of the latent ability to gallop. They are not infallible, however, and many an in-hand champion has reappeared under saddle as a four-year-old and confounded his erstwhile admirers with the realisation that he is capable of galloping just fast enough to keep himself warm. Few indeed are the young hunter champions who have been able to go on and sweep the board as the finished article.

Foals are the most difficult to judge at any time of their lives, particularly when looking into the future. It is not always the best mare who breeds the best-looking foal, quite often the reverse. In the show ring it is usually the most forward foal with presence and good movement that wins. A horse alters more when a foal than at any later stage of his life. It is possible to define a good set of limbs and sloping shoulder, and to see correct movement, though not many foals give a good show. Wobbly legs over at the knee and weak pasterns will in all probability strengthen up when older. Of course, you can always take the mare's conformation into account as well, especially if in doubt as to the foal's incorrectness: if the mare has the same fault you are more likely to have detected it correctly in the foal. Beware of going out and giving a high price for a champion foal as next year he may have grown out of recognition, while the foal you left behind was the one you should have had - for a smaller outlay.

Yearlings are slightly easier to judge and produce as their basic conformation will be there if you are knowledgeable enough to judge it. There are usually two sorts from which to choose. The first has been corn-fed like a fighting cock all winter and kept in a large, warm box. If he is a colt he will have been left uncut and will look rugged, and although he was probably only born the previous January, to many he looks like a two-year-old. The second has roughed it all winter and at best he has had a lean-to shelter to protect him from the worst of the weather. This yearling will be no match in the show ring for the former until he is three or four years old, because if foals are not looked after really well they take a considerable time to catch up.

It is possibly the good yearling which gets dragged from show to show after it has won a first prize or two that suffers the rigours of the show ring most in inexperienced hands by being over-shown, over-travelled and over-fed to its lasting detriment. The two- and three-year-old young hunters one sees shown are of all shapes and sizes from potential light-weights to heavyweights. Classes at the larger shows are usually split into colts and fillies. This in itself helps the judging considerably, and in any case it is an exceptional filly that beats a good colt.

The judge will be looking for the most correctly shaped animal that in his or her opinion will mature to the best in the class. The most deceptive things in the young horse are its shoulder and its outlook on life. The judge must visualise how it will look when a saddle and rider are on its back.

Producing youngstock correctly for the show ring is every bit as im-portant as any other class. One of the most difficult aspects for the owner-breeder who may well be an amateur is the condition that is required by many judges. However, as many owners get their animals over-fat as do not get them looking right. It is quite an art ensuring that they have just the right amount of condition on – condition that is flesh and muscle and not just fat – and, once this has been achieved, keeping it on when horses are travelling to shows in hot weather. When they are away from home in strange surroundings, they often stop eating and tuck up. Remember, too, that no matter how good you think your young hunter, you should always let it loose in the field every day for at least two to four hours. This prevents boredom and keeps the animal sane.

It does help, when showing two- and three-year-olds, to have them long-reined and mouthed by an expert if you are not capable of doing it yourself. This not only gives you much more control when showing them but also stops them being one-sided in the mouth later. Whatever type of bridle you decide to show your youngster in, remember to keep the bit high enough to stop it getting its tongue over, because once it learns this habit it is very hard to correct. The number of so-called knowledgeable experts to be seen at equestrian events with bits hanging out of their horses' mouths is always astounding.

All young horses should have great care taken of their feet, so have them checked regularly by your blacksmith. If you are showing two-year-olds, ask him to put a light shoe in front as this prevents them getting sore-footed on hard ground in the summer. Likewise have their teeth checked at the start of each season, together with a regular worming programme to ensure your young hunters' progress.

WORKING HUNTERS

The working-hunter classes are now some of the strongest and most popular competitions. At the large qualifying shows for the Horse of the Year Show, classes are divided into two weights: lightweight (up to 13 stone 7lb) and heavyweight (13 stone 7lb and over). A championship is held of the first and second of each section and the resulting champion and reserve qualify for the Horse of the Year Show. At other qualifying shows there is simply one open working-hunter class with the first and second animals going forward to the Horse of the Year Show. At the smaller, non-qualifying shows there is usually just an open working-hunter class for any height or weight.

Mr R. Shuck's champion working hunter, Jumbo Jet.

The definition of a show working hunter is a good-looking horse that jumps smoothly and quietly. He should be well schooled with correct symmetrical conformation, athletic movement and a good, level temperament.

Where many people make a mistake is in thinking that, because their animal jumps a gate or large hedge and ditch out hunting, they have a star working hunter. The same horse in a confined ring of unnatural fences often performs disastrously when asked to jump, say, six to ten fences of about 3ft 6in. to 3ft 9in. If they have not had experience of showing or some good tuition, many riders may find themselves at a disadvantage. To jump in a county-standard working-hunter class, a horse needs to have had a considerable amount of basic schooling and should be capable of jumping a Newcomer's course under British Show Jumping Association rules. It always seems a shame when a good-looking horse

Royal Harvest being schooled in preparation for his working-hunter classes.

enters the ring and has an appalling round because the owner has not taken enough trouble to school him at home first. In all probability the same horse out hunting is a star.

In selecting a horse for working-hunter classes, the choice is very wide indeed. Unlike the true show horse, the working hunter need not have a correct weight class. Obviously many top-class show animals go forward into the working-hunter classes towards the end of their showing career and a large number have come from the working-hunter class to reach great heights show jumping, eventing and racing. One recent example was the lovely brown 16.3 hh thoroughbred horse Andeguy, bred by Mr and Mrs Warcup of Berwick-upon-Tweed, broken by me and shown as a four-year-old to win, among other major shows, the Royal International. The following season he won many lightweight classes and the year after that he was Working Hunter of the Year besides winning some

Ex-show horse Andeguy and Olympic event rider Richard Meade performing a dressage test.

novice horse trials with Rosemary Thomson. He was then sold to Richard
Meade who evented him successfully and won the Boekelo Three-Day
Event Championship in Holland. HRH Princess Anne's Goodwill was a
former Working Hunter of the Year at Wembley and so too was Judy
Bradwell's Castlewellan.

Many of our top show hunters have gone on to make champion working hunters when properly schooled and educated to jump correctly.
Judging and selecting a horse to buy for a show working hunter is in fact
quite difficult as they come in all shapes and sizes. One must look for a
horse with natural presence and as correct in conformation as possible
with no apparent defects. When looking for a working hunter I like to
see a horse loose in a school to assess if it has any natural balance, to see
it jump something, however small, and if it has a natural jump. Most
horses can be taught, but the natural one is always at such an advantage
because it is easier to train and to work with.

Having selected your horse, you then have to teach it to jump in cold
blood. I usually start mine on the lunge jumping small fences with placing
poles at varying distances apart. This makes them think and teaches them
to use their neck and back. Some people school their horses loose but this
can make them wild and not careful enough: horses and ponies should be
taught to be careful and always jump correctly. The muscles then develop
in the right places, and the more correctly a horse jumps from the beginning, the fewer problems you will have to face later. When schooling
over fences, gymnastic exercises are most important and the amateur is
advised to seek help from a person more experienced in jumping if he or
she wants to succeed.

Before entering a county show with the real novice horse, you should
go to some small jumping shows and do as much clear-round jumping as
possible. In the winter months attend indoor jumping shows. This not
only schools the horse but also the rider. The main thing is to let your
horse see as many different types of fences as possible, for of course you
never know what you may be required to jump from show to show.
During a season you may be asked to jump water, bullfinches and
bounces, plus the usual water tanks and troughs, and have the occasional
footbridge to walk over. Teach your horse to go over its fences with a
good rhythm, to jump with its head lowered and neck and back arched
and be able to lengthen and shorten its stride before and after its fences.
Remember, too, that there is no substitute for practice away from home.

The working hunter should be the real workman of the hunters. It
should look fit, never fat, and horse and rider should seem as if they really
do mean business and are capable of going across country in any equestrian event. The Hunters Improvement Society marking system is 30 per

cent actual jumping, 20 per cent style and 50 per cent ride, presence and conformation. Jumping, therefore, counts considerably. Don't forget that the 20 per cent style makes a great deal of difference to the end result, so the importance of control in your jumping round is most essential. To have a pole down behind is obviously less serious than to have one in front, because if you were out hunting or riding across country it would in all probability give you a bad fall – and, of course, you do not win prizes lying on the ground. Judges give high ride marks for a good comfortable ride that is obedient to the aids and is the one they would like to take home to hunt or compete on. This class has many followers both from home and abroad looking for competition horses, so not only is it a good potential schooling ground, it is also an excellent shop window for breeders and owners wishing to sell their horses on at a later date.

THE LLOYDS BANK IN-HAND CHAMPIONSHIP

This is a championship class judged at about fifteen qualifying shows all round the country with a final at the Horse of the Year Show in October. The prize money is excellent and travelling and stabling expenses to London are paid for by Lloyds Bank. The aim is to find the supreme in-hand light horse or pony of the year. At Wembley the class is split into two: above 14.2 hh and under 14.2 hh., followed by a championship. It is a class that needs an expert horseman or horsewoman as a judge, for they can be faced with anything from a Shetland pony to a three-year-old hunter.

Many people say it is impossible to judge a yearling pony against a Welsh cob stallion, but if the person judging is knowledgeable, he or she should put up the animal which in his or her opinion is the most correct example of its type or is a picture of equine excellence. Unfortunately for the judge, he or she will be faced with animals of all shapes and sizes, ages and sexes from which to find the champion – no easy task. Judging is made all the more difficult when the animal they would most like to make their champion gives a very bad show and has to give way to another that is right on the day. This can be the result of showmanship and production or simply, as occasionally happens, because the best animal is lame and has to be dismissed.

Those eligible to compete in qualifying rounds are the respective champions from all the breeding sections at qualifying shows. These include the Arabs, the Welsh breeds, hunters, Cleveland bays, riding ponies and, of course, all of our native breeds. The judge then selects the champion on the day to go forward to London.

Invader, an Irish-bred three-year-old gelding, winner of many championships in hand, including his section of the 1983 Lloyds Bank final.

The Lloyds Bank Championship is one of the most hotly pursued classes in the show calendar and receives great public following and general publicity. It also gives breeders something to aim at, and if their stock is sold they can often follow their progress in Lloyds Bank competitions. Although some say these do not serve any useful purpose, many other knowledgeable people disagree and think themselves lucky that Lloyds Bank continues its sponsorship.

13

Hacks, Cobs and Riding Horses

In the old days there used to be two distinct types of hack. Before motorised horse transport there was the covert hack on which the wealthy owner would ride at a canter from his home to meet the foxhounds. At the meet he would change on to his hunter which his groom had previously walked over. The other type was called the park hack and on these ladies and gentlemen would ride in the city parks, such as the famous Rotten Row in London. In the last decade we have seen a revival in the popularity of hacks, particularly in the show ring, and we now have one basic type which is called the show hack.

The outstanding characteristics of the show hack are his grace, elegance and perfect manners. Quality is most important and can only be described by making a comparison with the quality seen in a really beautiful woman. Besides all these attributes the top-class show hack has that magical characteristic which is called presence, an impression of superiority hard to define and which compels and holds the attention of judges and spectators alike when the horse enters the ring. This element in the personality of a show horse is why one sometimes sees a technically correct and beautiful animal beaten by a character who seems to say to everyone, 'Look at me – I am the star.'

When judging for conformation, the hack must be as near perfect as possible. In eight out of ten cases a true hack will be a pure thoroughbred, although he must not exceed 15 hh for the small or 15.3 hh for the large class. A good animal should have about 8 inches of bone below the knee and be clean of its limbs with absolutely no unsoundness. You must avoid the weedy type of thoroughbred as this often lacks the necessary substance.

In the small hack class we now see quite a number of overgrown ponies or pony types. Many of these are light of bone, short-striding and short of front when ridden. Pony-bred hacks often look impressive when viewed outside the ring, especially when ridden by small ladies or teenagers. It is only when they are seen in the company of the true small hack type, which is a horse rather than a pony, or when they are ridden or judged by an experienced person, that the difference becomes obvious. Exhibitors often get very disappointed when they are pulled in at the top

of a line-up with a pony type and then are more often than not put down for the reasons described above.

When you have found an animal with the required quality and conformation, it should automatically follow that he will be a good and comfortable ride. The hack's action must be more spectacular than that of the hunter or riding horse and so the trot should be long and low with the potential to extend and point the toe when asked. The canter provides perhaps the greatest test of a show hack and should be noted for its balance, smoothness and rhythm. This is the proverbial hack canter which champions appear to do naturally. When it comes to action at the different paces, a mediocre animal will merely scratch along, while a champion flows effortlessly forward, reaching for the ground with his strides and using his shoulders to the full extent.

If he has correct natural paces, it is vitally important that a potential hack has the right schooling to develop further. Unfortunately, far too many animals are spoilt by being shown before they have been put through all the basic groundwork. The training of the show hack will follow the principles of dressage with the aim that he will carry his rider comfortably and quietly with free forward movement at all times. He must be 100 per cent responsive to the rider's aids and be light on the hands. The hack will be required to walk freely on a loose rein, trot elegantly, strike off into a collected canter extending as necessary, and come back quietly with no fuss to stand rock-still when asked. The object is to do all these things as obediently and quietly as possible. It will be clear that the more time and trouble one takes with the early training of the horse, the nearer perfect the end result is likely to be.

Sometimes a horse is submitted to brute force and ignorance in an effort to make it perform reasonably in the show ring, but a hack that is prepared in this way is most unlikely to have a successful long-term career. The hack that is taught correctly over a long period of time and not rushed into the ring will have acquired balance and suppleness in order to execute smooth changes of pace with the minimum amount of effort on the part of the rider. All this will require the sacrifice of many hours' time, but one simply cannot hurry or skimp on the training of the show hack. There are no short cuts to perfection.

The past masters in the art of showing hacks used to perform a rousing gallop in their individual show followed by a halt and unhurried rein-back, after which the horse was walked calmly back into line. Nowadays

Tomadachi, three times Champion Show Hack at the Royal International. The rider is correctly dressed for an evening performance.

A well turned-out winning combination in the ladies' hack class at the Royal International Horse Show.

the hack is never asked to gallop in the ring and the individual show does not exceed one and a half minutes. The performance should include a walk, trot, strike off to canter with a simple change of leg, halt and rein-back. The horse will demonstrate his obedience and responsiveness to the aids but there should be no anticipation of the next movement on the part of the horse.

There is a wealth of knowledge to be gained by watching a professional performance in these classes. The expert will give a show which appears simple but is as technically perfect as possible. Should the horse make a mistake, the rider will cover it up without a fuss and throughout the display will appear so calm and nonchalant that it will seem to be entirely without effort. One can also learn what *not* to do by watching a novice exhibitor who is likely to attempt a long and complicated show beyond his own or his horse's capabilities. In these cases the judge will often commence by watching politely but before long his patience and courtesy are exhausted so he turns away and asks the next competitor to come forward.

The hack classes have been generating a great deal of interest in the last few years. An abundance of enthusiasm is being shown by breeders, owners and riders of all ages, from children coming up from ponies to the more mature. It is encouraging that one may still be lucky enough to find a good animal unshown at a reasonable price, although obviously once a hack reaches the top of its class it can be very expensive to buy. Nevertheless, besides the professional showman, many of the dedicated amateurs in the showing world are having great fun with their hacks and there is still plenty of opportunity for them to reach the top on animals that they produce themselves at home.

THE COB

During the last five years show cobs have certainly come to the fore in popularity. One reason for the increasing interest in this type of animal is that cobs can be very useful all-rounders. Often they can be ridden by any member of the family for Pony Club, riding club or other equestrian activities as most of them are naturally good jumpers. They have always been considered suitable as an older person's conveyance for hacking and hunting but now many younger people are enjoying their cobs. Another reason for cobs' popularity is that they are relatively economical to keep as well as usually being easy to handle and good travellers.

However, although there has been a large increase in numbers, the standard has not always been high and it is quite difficult to find a quality riding cob that is always up to weight and of the correct height. The

show classes are now divided into two categories and the Show Hack and Cob Association's guide states that a lightweight should not exceed 15.1 hh and have at least 8½ inches of bone below the knee, while a heavyweight is classified to carry 14 stone or over at 15.1 hh. The true weight-carrying cob should have at least 9 inches of bone, with powerful hindquarters, but also a quality shoulder and head. The old saying that a show cob should have 'a head like a lady and a backside like a cook' is still an apt description of what one is seeking when looking for a cob to purchase. Mentally a cob should have a good, level temperament and excellent manners at all times, yet with a bright outlook, an abundance of presence, and gaiety in his movement.

Prior to 1945, cobs always had their manes hogged and their tails docked, but nowadays we see only the former. Occasionally they are shown with their tails plaited up to look more sturdy and perhaps to add to the overall character. My personal preference is for a neatly hogged mane with the tail left unplaited and cut precisely 2 inches below the point of the hock.

There are no particular advantages to any one colour in a cob, except perhaps what may be in fashion for the top animals at a given time. The animals to be avoided are the really common ones with round, soft bones and an action which makes them look as if they should be pulling a cart. You may find that people disguise a common horse by clipping out his head or even the whole of the body through the summer. Take care that the animal is not back at the knee or too straight at the shoulder with high knee movement as these faults will certainly mean that the horse is uncomfortable and jolting to ride. Look for a level and low, active movement which will make the ride smooth and the horse feel as easy to sit on as an armchair.

If you are thinking of buying a cob to show, it would be wise to have a vet check his respiration first because, being short in the neck and thick in the jaw, this type of horse is liable to have trouble in its wind and this will obviously make it unsuitable for the ring. Also, partly as a result of their conformation, too many cobs are very strong and tend to lean on their bridles or run away when asked to gallop. The good show cob will carry himself lightly and be responsive to the rider.

At the other end of the scale, you must avoid a horse that is too light of bone, for some people may have tried to jump on the cob bandwagon by taking the mane off the polo-pony type in the hope of selling him or trying to fox a judge. What you in fact are looking for is a heavyweight hunter in miniature.

The author on the champion lightweight show cob, Red Hill.

Mr W. Whale's Buzby, a champion heavyweight show cob, bred in Ireland by Green Whistle. This picture shows him after his winter holiday.

The same horse some six weeks later. This cob could be described as having 'a head like a lady and a backside like a cook', an old expression used when judging cobs. Note the tack is a workmanlike outfit with a wide noseband and a good comfortable saddle.

Two former champion show cobs: on the left, Roger Stack on twice Show Cob of the Year, Grandstand; and (right) David Tatlow on Huggy Bear, Show Cob of the Year when ridden by Roy Trigg.

As far as breeding is concerned, the cob is nearly always a freak and many combinations of stallion and mare height and weight may throw the cob type. Cobs are therefore not often intentionally bred but just seem to happen, and only an extreme optimist would predict that he had found the right formula to breed a champion. They have been bred in many parts of the country, particularly in Devon and Cornwall where there are still some of the good old short-legged mares that used to be called 'vanners'. Perhaps three-quarters of the cobs in the show ring today have been bred in Ireland – fairly often being by thoroughbred stallions out of an Irish draught or perhaps a Connemara mare. The cob with which I had most success, including winning the Show Cob of the Year title at Wembley in 1977, 1978 and 1979, was the bay gelding called Kempley. This horse was by the thoroughbred Salt Lake City out of a 14.3 hh cob-type mare. I brought him completely rough and untried from the dealer Bob Wooley. Kempley matured to be a most comfortable and naturally balanced horse with a low, flowing movement.

The cobs have now become an important section of the show classes at all the major shows. This achievement is largely due to the efforts of Miss Muriel Bowen, one of the doyennes of the cob world today, who has done a marvellous job in arranging sponsorship and promoting interest in these classes. Now we have not only lightweight and heavyweight classes but also an increasing number of classes for novices and amateur owner-riders.

Another personality in this field who seems to have a magic formula for finding, producing and riding show cobs is my friend of many years, Roy Trigg. His knowledge was very helpful to me when I started showing and every year he still finds cobs hidden in different parts of England and Ireland, all of which have a good pattern, are schooled to ride obediently and lightly, and show with great dash.

It is true that the old-fashioned quality cob is becoming a rarity. Those which have done well in the ring command quite high prices. There remains, as part of the magic of the cob world, the chance that one may still have the joy and satisfaction of finding a future champion rough in the field or undiscovered in the sale ring.

RIDING HORSES

The riding-horse classes have become very popular in recent years and attract a large number of entrants. They are usually divided into two sections: the small class for horses below 15.2 hh and the large which is for animals of 15.2 hh and over with no upper limit. Many small shows hold unaffiliated open classes where all the heights compete together, giving many owners the chance to show a good animal which, for one reason or another, could not otherwise fit into a specific class. An example of this would be a horse that is too small to be a lightweight hunter but lacks the final touch of class necessary for a hack.

The true show riding horse has quality and substance with enough bone below the knee to correspond with its height. The animal's conformation should, of course, be as correct as possible and he should not in any way be weedy or short of limb. The preferred movement is dead straight, long and flowing, but without that extravagant action associated with the hack. It would probably be right to say that one is looking for a combination of the characteristics found in a quality lightweight hunter and a hack. The riding horse must be up to sufficient weight to carry an average adult and be able to give that person a very well-schooled, comfortable ride. The horse should take a light hold of his bridle and be responsive to the rider's aids. He must also have the ability to gallop on and then pull up and stand still without any fuss or bother, so overall good manners are very important.

Originally in these classes horses were asked to jump a single fence in their individual show, but some people felt this was asking too much of the novices and four-year-olds which are often shown in this class, added to which some older riders were unhappy at being required to jump. Although some maintained that this was a sound practice in that it ruled out the hack that could not or would not jump, it was voted at a meeting of the British Show Hack and Cob Association to discontinue the requirement. The individual show lasting up to one and a half minutes now follows the same lines as that described for the hack but includes a gallop.

The judge in these classes will be looking for a horse that he would like to take out for a long ride in the country, in fact a horse that he really feels at home on. As mentioned before, the smooth ride of a good show horse accounts for a considerable amount of the total when a judge decides the final placings. The judge has the experience of riding many different animals and he will be looking for a certain standard according to the level of the show. Unfortunately, some exhibitors will be disappointed when their beautifully turned-out and presented horse is down the line because he gave a poor or even uncomfortable ride. This is always part and parcel of showing horses and exhibitors must accept it. If you disagree with the result for any reason, it is best to remember that in the riding-horse class, perhaps more than in any other, the judge has a very difficult task with so many different types to consider. Rather than criticise his assessment, use the experience gained to further your overall objectives.

The riding-horse class enables many people to show a wide variety of animals and can be useful at the smaller shows as a schooling exercise or

Tardy Eclipse, a 16 hh thoroughbred. This picture shows a fine example of a true type of show riding horse. He is 16 hh with 8 inches of bone, lots of presence and a very good mover.

to evaluate one's horse and its way of going when compared to others. A good-quality animal that is well schooled and produced to the owner's requirements will give many hours of pleasure both at home and in the show ring. As well as having many established supporters, these classes serve to whet the beginner's appetite to compete and then go on to other spheres in the equestrian world. With more and more shows putting on riding-horse classes and championships, and with sponsorship from commercial concerns on the increase, it seems certain that these classes will continue to grow and prosper.

14

Show Ponies

The standard of showing ponies today is as high as it has ever been. The top ten ponies at most major shows could in all probability be put in any order depending on their way of going on the day and the judges' personal preference. Breeders and producers leave very few stones unturned in their quest for championship honours. Long gone are the days when ponies could be produced out of the field to win, and even the small local shows have high-class exhibits. Today's ponies have, in many people's opinion, generally improved in their conformation in the last five years in that there are no longer so many that are very light of bone below the knee. Some new breeders and exhibitors were taking this lightness of bone as a sign of quality, but the good horsemaster knows the truth and considers these 'spider ponies' not show ponies. The few top ponies then were perhaps near-to-perfect models, but the misfits left a good deal to be desired with their weak hind legs and often doubtful temperaments. Recently quality seems to have been combined with good limbs at last. There is no point in having tiny heads and extravagant movement in front with the hind end, which should be the engine, trailing behind.

When breeding children's ponies, it is no easy matter to come up with the correct conformation, as well as the right temperament for young riders to show and manage, while keeping the all-important pony characteristics. Another difficulty when breeding and buying top-class ponies is to arrive at the right height, for a pony a quarter of an inch over height is often dwarfed by the larger animals when it is put into the higher height bracket.

Show ponies come under the auspices of the British Show Pony Society which was founded in 1949. The National Pony Society deals with the various breeding sections as well. Our English show ponies are the envy of the world, many being exported to ride, compete and breed in all corners of the globe. Some astronomical prices have been paid in the past, and will no doubt continue to be paid in the future, for a winning pony. Unfortunately, when some of these change riders and stables they do not continue their winning ways: producing the pony and rider as a partnership at the highest level is not an easy thing to do.

LEADING REIN

Show-pony classes begin with the leading-rein class which is for ponies suitable for a child rider of seven years old and under. The ponies, which must be four years old and over, have two height classes: one not to exceed 11.2 hh and the other of 11.2 to 12 hh. Lead-rein ponies have to be shown in snaffle bridles with the lead rein attached to the noseband. Judges in this class will be looking for a pony with correct conformation, good movement and a good front, and which is comfortable for the child to ride. A leading-rein pony short of front is not a good mount for a small child. Perfect manners in this class are important and in no way will a lapse of manners be allowed to pass.

You will find in this class two types of pony which each find favour with different judges. The first is the miniature blood pony, full of quality and good movement, and a real eyecatcher. This type often looks as if it might take flight if anything goes wrong, so that in many people's opinion it is not suitable as a leading-rein pony. The second type is the sturdier pony, probably of Welsh origin, with a good 'bombproof' temperament. Ideally, if you can find a pony between the two types, you are going to find favour with most judges.

In this class it often appears that the mothers and fathers are on parade more than the ponies and riders! Some of the outfits worn by the ladies would be more suitable for the dance hall or a society wedding than for leading a pony through the mud and slush on a wet show day. The object should be to look smart but not conspicuous while being dressed suitably for overhead and underfoot conditions. Gentlemen showing leading-rein ponies should wear a suit with a bowler hat. All ponies should be taught to go on the end of the lead-rein while the child has sufficient contact with the animal's mouth. In this class, as with all show classes, the overall picture counts towards success.

When producing the lead-rein pony, it is always advisable to give it some work on the lunge prior to being shown. This is because the light-weight young rider may easily be dislodged often through no fault of his own, if the pony shies or spooks in the ring.

FIRST-RIDDEN PONY

These ponies should be four years old and over and must not exceed 12hh. They are to be ridden by children nine years old and under, and again must be shown in snaffle bridles. These animals have to be shown off the rein and are required to walk and trot when all together. They are asked to canter when giving their individual show. The judge will be

A very neatly turned-out pony and rider for a first-ridden class.

looking for a well-mannered pony which goes quietly and freely forward with the child in charge of the situation.

Many ponies contest the lead-rein and first-ridden classes with different members of the family on board. It is usually the exception rather than the rule that the top winning lead-rein ponies are as successful in first-ridden classes. On the whole, the good first-ridden pony is more forward-going and has a scopier outlook together with a longer stride.

12.2 HH

The 12.2 hh show-pony class is for ponies four years old and over which do not exceed 12.2 hh, ridden by children of twelve years old and under. In this class judges will expect a quality, well-mannered pony which, in their opinion, is suitable for the younger child to show.

One of the most outstanding ponies during the last few years has been Dr and Mrs Gilbert Scott's Arden Vol-au-Vent of Creden. A pony gelding by Creden Valhalla out of Arden Bronze, he was exceptional in his conformation, quality, movement and temperament and was everyone's ideal type of top-class 12.2hh show pony. He remained to the fore for many seasons.

Every parent and child's dream: a lap of honour for Antonia Sandison on 12.2 hh Harmony Bubbling Champagne at Wembley, 1983.

12.2 hh ponies can and do vary in type as some have a predominance of Welsh blood in them. The ones with too much native blood are inclined to be thick in the shoulder and lack the free-going movement required. The top 12.2 hh pony should be more refined than the first-ridden and should include a change of rein at the canter and a few strides of gallop. Judges will, of course, be looking for ponies that are mannerly and well schooled.

13.2 HH

The 13.2 hh show-pony class is for ponies exceeding 12.2 hh but not exceeding 13.2 hh, ridden by children of fourteen years and under. It is one of the strongest classes to win with some of the most correct and beautifully bred ponies in it. In this class breeders seem to have found the right blend of quality while retaining all the necessary pony chacteristics. Riders in this age group, too, seem more suitably mounted and retain the good overall appearance that means so much to the judge's eye.

In this height group one of the most outstanding ponies for many years was Cathryn Cooper's chestnut mare Holly of Spring, which was by that illustrious ridden pony Gem's Signet out of Penhill Finola. At this height the judges will be looking for ponies that really cover the ground and which are polished and fluent in their individual shows.

Cathryn Cooper on champion 13.2 hh Holly of Spring.

14.2 HH

The 14.2 hh show-pony classes are for ponies exceeding 13.2 hh and not exceeding 14.2 hh, ridden by children of sixteen years and under. Of all the ponies, the 14.2 hh is the most difficult to find, and breeders' opinions differ as to what constitutes a good example. Many ponies around the 14 hh height usually retain the pony characteristics but lack scope and size. When up to full height, they tend to go too horsy. With the introduction of the juvenile rider's and the pony of hunter-type classes this year, it is now more essential than ever that judges, breeders and exhibitors should try to keep to the pony type of 14.2 hh show pony. This pony should possess correct limbs and a good sloping shoulder, together with the all-important pony head. It should be a forward-going animal, bold in its outlook and capable of being ridden by children up to sixteen years of age. It should be able to gallop really well and give individual shows that are completely controlled and a pleasure to watch.

15 HH

The 15 hh pony exceeds 14 hh but does not exceed 15 hh. Riders are between the ages of fourteen and eighteen. This class now caters for many misfits and experts say that when a pony is over 14.2 hh he is not a pony.

Camilla Shuck on 14.2 hh Keston Brown Sugar. A grand pony, beautifully turned out, with its rider correctly dressed for show-pony classes.

It is a class that helps children make the difficult transition from ponies to larger horses. It is a good class for overgrown 14.2 hh ponies or small hacks of the pony type.

The majority of children's pony sidesaddle classes are now for ponies up to 15 hh of four years and over, ridden by young people of seventeen years and under. As in all classes these ponies have to give an individual show when asked. Again, judges will be looking for type and the suitability of the animal to carry its rider sidesaddle, the overall picture being very important. The large saddle and large child on a small pony do not compare to the young rider and mount who are well suited to each other.

Those keen on the now-popular sidesaddle riding have the added advantage of being able to compete in junior sidesaddle equitation classes. During the season several shows have a class for pony pairs. Ponies should not exceed 15 hh and riders must be seventeen years old or under. The animals are ridden side by side and judged together on matching looks, turnout and way of going as a pair.

NOVICE SHOW PONIES

Some shows have 12.2 hh, 13.2 hh and 14.2 hh novice pony classes. The smaller shows with less time available or insufficient entries to warrant three have just one class for ponies up to 14.2 hh. The permitted age group of the riders is the same as for open show-pony classes. A novice pony is four years old and over and must not have a first prize of £5 or over in affiliated British Show Pony Society classes. Such an animal that wins an open class with a first prize of £5 or over, or an open pony championship, is immediately classed as an open show pony for the rest of its showing life.

Three-year-old ponies can be shown from July 1st of that year but only in the novice classes. All three-year-old and novice ponies have to be shown in snaffle bridles, and in all show-pony classes spurs are forbidden. There are some exemptions to the novice show-pony rule which are listed in the current rule book. In judging novice classes, judges will be looking for the potential top-class pony and will allow a certain amount of greenness in the way of going and to the general finish of the pony.

PONY OF HUNTER TYPE

In 1984 a new class came to the fore: the pony of hunter type. This seemed to fill a gap for children and breeders not necessarily interested in producing a top-class show pony. It has also given an opening for ponies which will later go on and make top-class working-hunter event ponies. The ideal pony for this class will have the correct conformation and be a miniature of our show hunter.

There are three height groups; not to exceed 13 hh, for children of fourteen years and under; not to exceed 14 hh for children of sixteen years and under; and not to exceed 15 hh for children of eighteen years and under. Judges in this section are not chosen from the BSPS show-pony panel but from the working-hunter pony panel. It is to be hoped that these judges will soon be able to assess a standard type, as obviously in the early days of this class ponies will vary from the weedy blood-type to those bordering on commonness. The pioneering classes seen in 1984 were well supported and several ponies of the correct type came to the fore.

Top Hat, as he arrived to start the season. Three months later this woolly little person became Champion Hunter Pony at the Royal International.

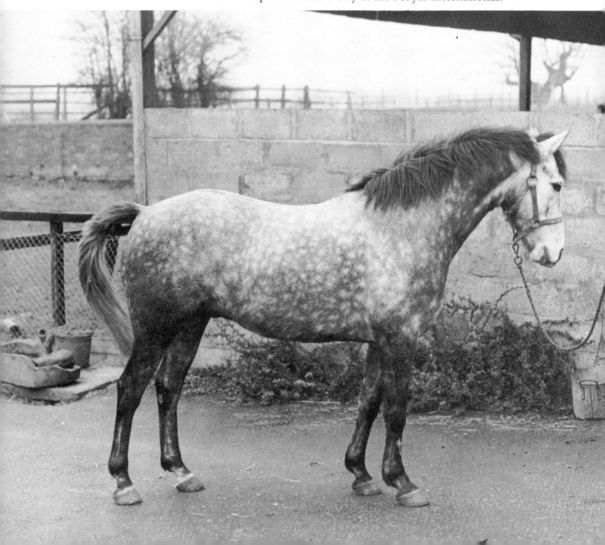

The same pony, six weeks later, clipped and trimmed prior to winning the championship at Stoneleigh spring show. Top Hat stands 15 hh and is by a thoroughbred out of a mare by Valentino.

Top Hat again, receiving his prize at the Royal International, 1984.

WORKING-HUNTER PONIES

Working-hunter ponies are now a most popular class. This is possibly due
to the fact that competitors can generally follow the judging quite easily
under the present excellent marking system which seems to meet with
most people's approval. Marks are awarded out of 100, as follows:

Phase one –	jumping	50
	style and manners while jumping	10
Phase two –	conformation and freedom of action	30
	manners	10
		Total: 100

Penalties:

Phase one –	jumping knock-down	10
	first refusal	15
	second refusal	20
	third refusal	disqualification
Fall of pony or rider in either phase		20

The standard requirements of a working-hunter pony are difficult to
pinpoint. The ideal is a quality pony of hunter type, a deep animal on
four good, sound limbs. A show-pony type, short of bone below the knee
with a plain head, will not do. The pony needs to be free-moving with
a bold outlook and must, with its rider, present not only a happy, controlled picture but also look capable of going across country.

The working-hunter pony class does not need the true flashy movement
of the show pony but should be a good, straight, level mover. Some
judges will even accept 'handsome is as handsome does', as the old saying
goes, meaning that if the pony is on the plain side but well schooled and
performs well, it will be preferred to the pretty animal that does not jump
fluently. Performance in a working-hunter pony class should always be
the deciding factor. The jumping phase is completed first, during which
judges will be looking for an animal that jumps fluently, not rushing its
fences or requiring a lot of effort to get it to go. The pony should go on
an even rhythm and be able to lengthen and shorten its stride with the
rider in complete control and enjoying the round. Those required for the
second phase – usually the ones who went clear in phase one – then
complete individual shows and are given their conformation mark. Their
marks are then added together to find the final placings.

The classes for working-hunter ponies are: cradle stakes – for ponies
not exceeding 12 hh, with riders of nine years and under; nursery stakes
– for ponies not exceeding 13 hh, with riders of eleven years and under;

working-hunter ponies – not exceeding 13 hh, with riders of fourteen years and under; working-hunter ponies – exceeding 13 hh but not exceeding 14 hh, with riders of sixteen years and under; working-hunter ponies – exceeding 14 hh but not exceeding 15 hh, with riders of eighteen years and under.

Novice classes are also catered for at many shows, particularly during the winter months. A novice working-hunter pony must not have won a first prize of £5 or over on 1st October of the previous year in a British Show Pony Society affiliated class. All ponies have to be four years and over and, as in all BSPS children's classes, no spurs are allowed.

The goal of working-hunter pony enthusiasts is the Peterborough Championships, held annually at Alwalton early in September. Ponies have to qualify during the season for these championships, in which they should be well prepared to meet some formidable courses, usually much larger and more difficult than they have encountered all season.

RIDING-PONY BREEDING

The riding-pony breeding sections at most of the large shows are full now of some of the finest ponies one could find anywhere. Only possibly at the real tail end would you find an unexceptional pony or two. Most of our pony breeding stock goes back to the legendary Pretty Polly, a chestnut mare bred in Southern Ireland by Mrs S.A. Nicholson in 1945, sired by the grey Arab Nazeel out of a Welsh mare called Gypsy Gold. Pretty Polly was later sold to the late Mr A. Deptford of Peterborough, where in the hands of Davina Lee-Smith she swept the board for three seasons as a ridden 14.2 hh (although she measured only 14 hh), twice being Show Pony of the Year. She was mated to various stallions, including the legendary Bwlch Valentino, who in turn sired Bwlch Zephyr out of the show-pony mare Miss Minnette. Bwlch Zephyr was the sire of yet another even more illustrious pony, Bwlch Hill Wind.

The pony stallion which has placed such a hallmark on our ponies was Bwlch Valentino, the grey 14.2 hh pony stallion owned by Mr and Mrs I.V. Eckley and bred by the late Mrs Nell Pennel. He was sired by Valentine (who was sired by Malice) out of Bwlch Goldflake. Valentino has sired innumerable champion ponies and is in the pedigree of so many more. He was remarkable both for his correct conformation and his wonderful movement, temperament and soundness, which allowed him to be regularly ridden well into his old age, shepherding round the Eckleys' farm and stud.

Valentino's two well-known descendants, Bwlch Zephyr and Bwlch Hill Wind, belonged to that highly respected judge and breeder, Miss E.

Ferguson. Hill Wind sired the famous Gem's Signet, the chestnut belonging to Amanda Sangan who won so many championships. He in turn, before being gelded, sired Holly of Spring, the undisputed 13.2 hh champion pony mare.

In recent years many fine animals have come from studs up and down the country, and with so many breeders hoping to produce a future champion it must always be in everyone's mind that no two judges will agree on what constitutes the perfect child's pony. The breeders, however, must be admired for their devotion in continuing to strive for near-perfection. The breeding of 12.2 hh and 13.2 hh seems close to perfection, but in the 14.2 hh class it is still very difficult to get the pony with correct height together with true pony characteristics as so many are horsy types.

As with all youngstock it is unwise to over-show ponies, for without doubt when their ridden days arrive many in-hand champions fade away as a result of being forced in their youth. If the future ridden pony can be found unshown, so much the better, as most experts believe that this is how an animal keeps its natural presence. Without doubt it usually has a better mouth, because too much in-hand showing does make a pony one-sided.

The classification of breeding show ponies at the leading shows starts with brood mares in height sections: not exceeding 12.2 hh, not exceeding 13.2 hh and not exceeding 14.2 hh. Foals out of the above classes also have a class of their own. At the smaller shows schedules usually state 'riding-pony brood mares open not to exceed 14.2 hh'. In the youngstock classes the sections are: yearling colt, filly or gelding not to exceed 12.2 hh at maturity, not to exceed 13.2 hh, and not to exceed 14.2 hh. The same height specifications apply to two- and three-year-olds.

Youngstock entries in classes with restricted height limits are at most shows measured outside the ring. No official measurement certificates are given to animals under four years old. The required heights for breeding classes are as follows:

> ponies not to exceed 14.2 hh at maturity: yearlings not to exceed 13.3 hh, two-year-olds should not exceed 14 hh, and three-year-olds should not exceed 14.1 hh.
> ponies not to exceed 13.2 hh at maturity: yearlings not to exceed 12.3 hh, two-year-olds not to exceed 13 hh, and three-year-olds not to exceed 13.1 hh.
> ponies not to exceed 12.2 hh at maturity: yearlings not to exceed 11.3 hh, two-year-olds not to exceed 12 hh, and three-year-olds not to exceed 12.1 hh.

It is always wise to accustom youngstock to the measuring stick regularly at home so that, when away at a show, they will have no fear of a stranger wielding one. If your animal is up to height, it must be relaxed for the official to measure it correctly.

15

Judges

Exhibitors must realise that when they bring an animal into the ring to be judged, no matter how large or small the show, they have brought it there for the judge's opinion. Judges in England are not paid for their services, but many of them have a lifetime's knowledge of horses and ponies. It must be remembered, too, that no matter how right or wrong, every person has a different opinion and method of judging. There will be some who are conformation perfectionists and others who, when assessing ride, give far greater importance to the horse's feel and way of going. This, of course, is what makes showing the attraction it is. If there was never any difference of opinion among judges, exhibitors would cease to do the show circuit, especially as the cost of producing and travelling nowadays has reached such a high level.

When a judge accepts an invitation, he does so on the understanding that he is there to place the exhibits in the order of preference. It is the judge's opinion *on the day* that is important – on another day the same judge may for some reason or another place them differently. Remember that the judge's decision is final, but only in the case of lameness or bad manners should they refuse to place an exhibit.

Judges too should remember that they should take their job seriously, for many exhibits are valuable and have cost a great deal of time and money to produce. As results are published world wide, it can detract many thousands of pounds from the value of a horse if it is unfairly judged or put down unnecessarily at a show because of some person's whim.

We in England have some of the most knowledgeable people on our horse and pony judging panels, but every year it becomes more and more difficult to find young people with the time and experience to do the job. It is a matter of considerable concern that through old age and ill health so many of the older judges are fading out and few young ones are coming on to fill their places. With more people riding now for pleasure than ever before, it would seem a simple matter to add to the judges' panel. However, although the committees responsible do their best to find fresh blood, few new names are added to the lists. Junior or learner panels have been tried with a certain amount of success, but some judges are rather shy of divulging their honest opinions to strange young people as their remarks are not always treated in the strictest confidence. It is one thing to judge an animal on its own in your own time but quite a different matter to be presented with a class of perhaps twenty animals to be judged in one hour. Obviously experience comes into its own then, but the only way to learn is by going with an older judge into the ring to gain the experience.

During the judging of in-hand classes the animals are presented at the walk, making full use of the ring. After an initial walk round, at which the judge has noticed the animal whose presence and outlook he prefers, the showman comes into his own in presenting his animal correctly. The judge then asks the steward to call the animals in his initial order of preference. Occasionally some judges call them in as they walk round, though in my opinion this is of no help and much changing around has to be done. If it is a very large class, the back row may be called in first.

The right way to stand a horse or pony for assessment by a judge. It is also the correct view for taking a photograph. Note correct limbs, short back, good outlook; this horse may be short in neck, if ultra critical.

This is often done at shows in Ireland. If the animals in the back row are of poor quality, they may, if they wish, leave the ring, which in fact saves exhibits having to stay unnecessarily in bad or very hot weather. This point is often overlooked by new exhibits and can cause friction, but provided the judge has looked at them and it is a very large class, it serves no purpose to stay.

The next stage is to look at the remaining animals. They are brought forward one at a time for the judge to inspect and then asked to walk away and trot back so that he can assess their action. The whole class is then asked to walk round and the steward, at the judge's wish, calls them in in the order chosen by the latter. The judge will have placed them in his order of preference.

If on this occasion your horse or pony behaved well and, in your opinion, gave a good show but was unplaced, remember that there is always another judge and another day. Do not go outside and complain. Take your medicine and remember that judges do not ask you – or certainly should not have asked you – to compete. Losing is part of showing, and if you cannot stand the pressure you should find another pastime. To say a judge is blind or deaf to a horse's fault is no way to behave and this kind of unpleasantness outside the ring unfortunately gives showing a bad name. Disappointed exhibitors sometimes verbally abuse a judge if their animal has previously done a lot of winning and perhaps for reasons unknown suddenly has an off day. The judge then has the courage of his convictions and quite rightly places the animal down.

If you happen to know a particular judge quite well, do not be familiar with him in the ring but treat him as you would a stranger. It is most embarrassing for the judge and other competitors if you address him by his first name in the ring. You will be watched by other people who will immediately conclude that there is favouritism if there appears to be familiarity of any kind. If you speak, just say: 'Yes, Sir' or 'No, Sir'.

The ride usually required of a hunter, hack or cob differs from judge to judge. First, the hunter, when ridden by the judge, will be required to walk, trot, canter and gallop. The judge will want a calm, generous ride, the horse going well up to his bridle and answering to the basic leg aids. A horse that rushes off in his transitions or fails to come back to you in a smooth mannerly way is always marked down. An alert, generous way of going freely forward, covering the ground easily, is what most people require. A horse that shows no waywardness or vice of any kind and which is neither a slug nor too sharp – in other words, an animal of character and individuality – is the one to find most favour. Hunters in particular tend to get ring-crafty and start hanging in and cutting the corners of the ring – attributes that most judges hate to find in a show ride. Nor do they like show animals to be fresh and above themselves. The judge will also be looking for smoothness and obedience in his ride, and often this is where a horse pulled in high is then put down, especially if the animal is good-looking but still fails to give the ride required by the judge in question.

In a cob the judge will be looking for a ride of a well-schooled nature. The horse should not take too much hold, a fault of most cobs which tend to lean and rush off into the gallop. They can and should be active, able really to cover the ground, and then come back and stand rock-still until told to move off again. They should rein back the necessary number of strides and canter forward if asked to, all in the pleasant, cheerful, cocky way that the best cobs seem able to do. It is in the ride that the common bone-shaker is soon found out.

The show hack, through force of circumstances as explained earlier, is now purely a show animal. The judge will require obedience, smoothness and a temperament of unfailing generosity. Anticipated movements are always marked down, a failing found in a large number of over-schooled hacks. An animal which goes forward freely with a very light contact and which, in fact, carries itself is the one most judges particularly like and will always try to put up. In small hacks one gets a lot of tippety short-striding pony-type rides which fail to cover the ground, a fault which is only discovered by the judge when he rides the animals, and this is where exhibitors can be so disappointed.

It must be remembered that many show animals, especially light and small hunters and hacks, may have been ridden almost entirely by ladies. Because of this a judge often finds when he rides them that, unaccustomed to his extra weight, longer coat tails and different riding styles, they tend to put their backs up for the first few minutes. Therefore, if a judge is wise, he will keep a contact with the animal's mouth from the moment he sits in the saddle. Under these circumstances it is wisest to sit slightly behind the horse and maintain impulsion, thus preventing a buck or a kick and the occasional unseating.

The wide range of saddles found on animals in the show ring, particularly on hacks, is rather alarming. These might be jumping saddles, pony or cut-back show saddles and even continental dressage saddles.

It is usually very difficult for a judge to get a good comfortable ride from a horse, especially a novice, if he is riding short with his bottom right out of the saddle. As an old friend of mine, a Yorkshire farmer, once said, 'Yer can't judge 'osses without yer ass int' saddle.' It is therefore fairly clear that judges find it hard to ride in the cut-forward saddle, tipped up at the back with a deep seat. The best types of saddle are well-worn hunting ones or Champion and Wilton saddles.

Judges' requirements as to ridden show ponies vary greatly. Most people will agree, however, that the show pony must exhibit quality and should not be light-boned and weedy. It should have correct conformation, showing true pony character, and the most perfect manners. It must also be suitable for the size of rider that the schedule allows. A good judge will be able to see that a corned-up blood pony requires an experienced child rider to cope with it. However, some of the top-prize-winning children today would leave many a professional showman standing with regard to know-how and ringcraft.

Of all the classes today, pony classes are probably the hardest to judge. There is always the problem of misbehaviour, often behind the judge's back. Exhibitors must remember that a buck occurs when all four of the animal's feet leave the ground with the head below the withers and not when a pony, particularly a 13.2 or 14.2 hh, shakes his head, probably simply because he is full of the joys of spring. This animal should not be put down to a dozy beast who never puts a foot wrong.

16

The Horse of the Year Show

The Horse of the Year Show was originally started by a band of keen horsemen in September 1949, at Harringay in London, under the directorship of Sir Mike Ansell. It was then and still is run under the auspices of the British Show Jumping Association, to whom all the profits go. Few people at its inception would have thought that it would aspire to become possibly the best and greatest indoor horse show in the world. Its timing and organisation is second to none. Seats are booked from year to year and, without prior booking, it is virtually impossible to buy tickets for the last three days. And it is not surprising, for this show has such a wonderful atmosphere – a kind of content, end-of-season feeling. It is the climax of the year and obviously exhibitors, riders, grooms and public alike all want to attend. It is undoubtedly every showing person's ambition to win the prestigious title of Horse or Pony of the Year.

In order to enter the Horse of the Year Show one has to qualify at one of the many shows nominated by the Horse of the Year Show committee and the various breed societies. The qualifications vary from one breed section to another. In some cases the class winner goes through and in others it may be the champion and reserve. Often if the winner of a class has already qualified for Wembley, the second and third place animals go through. The regulations covering qualifications vary from year to year depending on the number of exhibits required by the committee in the preliminary judging. This is mainly because a tight schedule is enforced during the Show week and possible delays must be strictly avoided.

The preliminary judging at Wembley usually takes place in the morning and is quite different from other shows in that a points system is used. It is organised as follows:
1. The whole class appears before the two judges showing the various paces required.
2. The class then splits into two: half remains for one judge to ride, whilst the other is judged for conformation, action in hand and soundness of limb. The sections then change places.
3. In the next phase, where the judges are looking for presence, the first eight or nine horses required for final judging are selected from approximately twelve with the highest marks after the conclusion of the earlier assessments.

Conformation judging at Wembley, taking place outside on concrete. On the left a veterinary surgeon; on the right, the judge, Mr A. Steward.

The proportions of marks in the phases are as follows:

Conformation, action in hand and soundness of limb	40%
Ride	40%
Presence	20%

The final marking for all phases is based on the place order. In the event of a tie in the total marks the judges may award part of a mark in the presence phase.

The conformation judging is where some people come unstuck because it takes place on a concrete surface, so exhibitors do not have the benefit of grass to disguise poor conformation of the feet as they do at other shows. After the animals have been assessed for conformation they are then trotted in hand to display their movement. A true, straight action and soundness of limb is required and any faults soon become evident. A veterinary surgeon is always available if there is any doubt as to a horse's soundness and his decision is final. Each year a number of exhibits are eliminated or 'spun' at this examination because of lameness or from being unlevel. Many a tear may be shed at this stage but the decision of the judge or the vet must be accepted.

In the judge's ride the exhibits are assessed for training, smoothness of ride and general suitability. In the case of hacks and ponies they each give an individual show.

Next, the animals are asked to walk round whilst the judges sort them out in some order of preference and award them marks for presence. Eight or nine are then selected to go forward to the final judging, which takes place either in the afternoon or evening. This is, of course, the ambition and indeed the highlight for the exhibitors. To reach this stage is in itself quite an achievement when one considers how many fail to get there.

The finalists are then told when to report to the outer collecting ring. This will be at least thirty minutes before they are asked to go forward to the inner collecting ring. Once the class ahead leaves the main arena the next is called in and this is the time when most people become nervous. Even the most seasoned compaigners feel the excitement and anticipation which this atmosphere creates and which invariably affects the horses.

The procedure in the final judging is the same as in any show but sometimes if the placings are difficult to separate an exhibitor may be asked to give an individual show. Misbehaviour of the animal at this stage is strictly penalised. Once the prizes are given the winner is pulled out ahead of the line to stand alone while the rest of the class leaves the ring. The winner then proceeds on a lap of honour under the spotlight to the cheers of the audience, always a thrilling moment. If a section has a championship for which the first two places qualify, then the winner and runner-up go forward to compete in a later contest when, after an individual show, the overall champion is announced.

To prepare an animal for the Horse of the Year Show, which traditionally always takes place in early October, requires great technique. The horse must arrive in top-class condition and be going quite brilliantly, which is not easy at a time when horses and ponies are changing their coats and may be going off their best form as a result of a long hard season of competitions. As well as perfect fitness and turnout a level state of mind is essential, as the busy environment and lively atmosphere of a large indoor show affects even the quietest animal – something which many potential champions have found to their misfortune. Conversely, an animal which otherwise lacks that extra presence and sparkle will often produce an exceptional performance in the Wembley arena. These exhibits are often referred to as London types rather than outdoor, county show animals.

Firstly, having hopefully the right amount of condition on your exhibit – fit and firm not fat and flabby – it is essential to have kept your horse warm in September with extra rugs when the nights grow cooler. Some stables even go to the trouble of putting infra-red heating in the boxes and leaving a light on night and day to make the animal think it is still midsummer. If the animal's coat does come through and is long enough it could be clipped, in which case a complete clip should be carried out about ten days prior to the show day. This will allow a nice new coat to grow in time for it to look at its best on the required day. The only possible exceptions are chestnuts which can look worse if they are a pale colour and are therefore best left unclipped. Whatever colour your horse or pony, the ideal is not to clip before Wembley. If, however, you do choose to clip great care must be taken to ensure that the animal is warm at all times otherwise his coat will go starey and the effect is disastrous. A few days before the show thorough trimming of manes, tails and heels and a good shampoo should be carried out. Most important of all is the shoeing. It still amazes me, year after year, that people arrive at shows with their exhibit in need of shoeing. Nowhere is correct shoeing more important than on the concrete at Wembley. Do get your farrier to inspect your animal in action *before* he puts on new shoes or in the case of ponies, plates so that he may correct any unlevelness. It is advisable to have any shoeing done about four to ten days before the animal is shown to give the shoe a chance to settle onto the foot.

A very important aspect of all show classes is the way in which a horse behaves in hand. He must come out before the judge and be taught to stand properly and to run out in hand correctly. Many points can be won or lost at the Horse of the Year Show in this phase. Careful preparation at home will benefit not only the horse but the exhibitor as well.

Exhibits need to be extra quiet and well worked-in prior to their judging as the last thing you want is a horse or pony too fresh. Exhibits are better over- than under-worked because once in the arena I can assure you there is nothing you can do to keep them out of the way of the others. Usually they are nose to tail when they are going round.

Tips for Exhibitors Making their Wembley Debut

It will be necessary to take with you extra bedding if you intend to stable your horse the night before you compete. This must be either peat moss or shavings because straw is considered a fire risk; neither is provided free by the organisers. The weather at this time of year is unpredictable so take extra rugs and bear in mind that the temporary stabling at Wembley will not be as warm as at home. If you have a hood this can be used to keep the horse's coat down but take care that it fits correctly otherwise it may go into the horse's eye.

View of the outside showground at Wembley.

Outdoor ring.

Security is always a worry at places such as Wembley where your horsebox may be parked some distance from your stable and a lot of leg work may be involved. Your tack and equipment should therefore be kept in your lorry for safety reasons. If you take a bicycle with you be sure to keep it locked up. Remember, you are in London, not out in the sticks.

Preparing for a class in the temporary stables. Note wire grilles, ideal for keeping horses in and for preventing too much attention from the many visitors.

Exercising is carried out either in an outdoor sand arena, which can be very deep and holding but is available at all times, or in the main ring. This is free only between 5 a.m. and 7 a.m. with normally one hour allowed for each section. I strongly advise riders to ride in the indoor arena to familiarise their horses and ponies in preparation for their class. If you have not shown at Wembley before you will want to know how

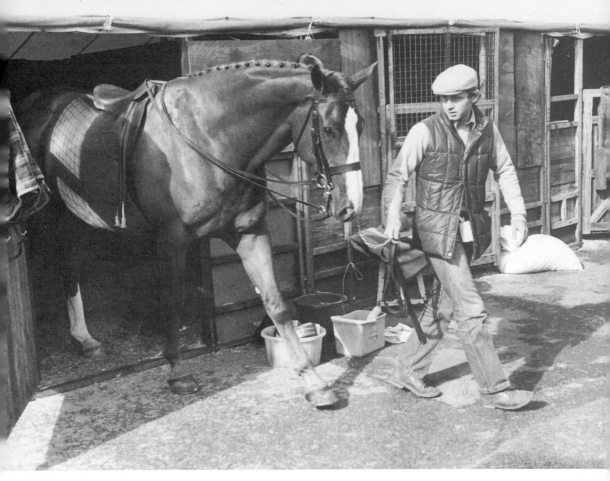

Ready for the off. Seabrook leaves his stables early in the morning, hours later to become 1984 Show Hunter of the Year.

your horse is likely to behave. Take no chances and work him thoroughly.

Having worked your horse early in the morning on the day of your class let him cool off quietly and then give him a small feed. After this the groom or whoever is looking after the animal, should set to and groom the horse like it has never been groomed before, paying a great deal of attention to every detail. Once this is done the horse can be tacked up and given a final polish. Depending on the individual animal's temperament the exhibits generally need to be ready about half an hour before the time they are required for the class. The rider, who himself must be absolutely spotless, should then ride him down to the collecting ring and await the steward's instructions as to when to enter the ring.

If you are fortunate enough to make it to the final your horse or pony can be returned to his stable and, when appropriate, produced for the

final judging. The preparation should be repeated just as meticulously and the rider will need to change into the appropriate dress for the perform-ance.

Those who watch the Horse of the Year Show on the television or from the comfort of a ringside seat will have little idea of the time and trouble which goes into preparing an exhibit. This is sometimes made more difficult by wet and windy conditions outdoors, but no matter, the horse must be immaculate by the time he reaches the ring.

The Finale

This chapter would not be complete without mentioning the famous last night of the Horse of the Year Show. It is a memorable and unique occasion when all the personalities and competitors who have been in-volved throughout the week, parade together in the Cavalcade. The Household Cavalry trumpeters sound a fanfare and the show is then drawn to a close by Dorian Williams reading Ronald Duncan's *The Tribute to the Horse*. This is one of the most moving renditions I have ever heard and it makes a fitting end to the show and to this chapter.

> Where in this wide world can man find
> nobility without pride, friendship without envy,
> or beauty without vanity? Here, where grace is
> laced with muscle and strength by gentleness confined.
> He serves without servility, he has fought
> without emnity. There is nothing so powerful,
> nothing less violent; there is nothing so quick,
> nothing more patient.
> England's past has been borne on his back.
> All our history is his industry. We are his heirs,
> he our inheritance.
> The Horse!

A champion leaves under spotlight.

17

Do's and Don'ts

Never lead a horse or pony with a rack chain or, in fact, any type of chain, because if frightened it may well pull the chain through your hand. So many people have lost fingers in this way or experienced serious hand injuries, particularly in the case of chains with metal clips. This point specially applies when loading horses at shows.

Never leave a rack chain with a clip hanging in a stable. Many horses and ponies over the years have suffered agonies from getting them caught up in their nose, mouth or lips while playing with them, have had to have expensive veterinary treatment and have been out of work for some time.

Never tie animals up too close to the ground. There is always a risk of their getting their necks under the rope and getting hung up. If they do they often panic and cannot free themselves, making it necessary to cut them free.

Never tie animals up to moveable or lightly fixed objects, for example drainpipes or small garden gates, because if they pull back the whole thing can go with them. I have witnessed several serious accidents at shows with animals racing round with objects attached to them. You must always remember that, when frightened, horses and ponies career about and can crash into vehicles, sometimes injuring themselves fatally.

Never turn show horses out together with hind shoes on. You can guarantee that sooner or later one will get kicked, usually in a vital spot, which could render it useless for the show ring.

Never leave bottom bolts or latches undone on bottom stable doors, because if the horse rolls or paws at the door, there is a great danger of the door opening enough to let his foot out so that it gets caught like a rat in a trap. In such an instance very serious damage and scarring can occur.

Never leave a hay net hanging at too low a level so that a horse or pony could get caught up in it. If it happened at night, the animal could be there for some considerable time and permanent tendon damage could result.

Never leave shoes on for longer than four weeks, even if they appear tight, as they may well be in at the heels and cause corns. The horn of the hoof never stops growing.

Never leave a horse in the ring with a groom. It is considered very bad manners except, of course, in cases of real emergency. Exhibitors have been seen to leave just to chat to outsiders.

Never get into conversation with a judge, for it leads to bad feelings and often embarrassment on everyone's part. Just politely answer any questions you may be asked.

Never ride without a hard hat or crash cap.

Never ride a horse or pony bareback on the road. An ex-groom of mine was killed at her home one weekend while riding a horse back from its field in this way.

Never ride in summer shoes or shoes with no heel, because if you get caught up or fall there is a great risk of your foot going through the stirrup and of your being dragged.

Never ride in nickel stirrup irons as, if you have a fall, particularly on the road, the soft metal will close on your foot and you will be dragged, unable to free yourself.

Never ride with cheap nickel-buckled stirrup leathers, especially when jumping or hunting, as they will easily break. In fact, always check buckles and leathers for wear regularly as breakages are common. One well-known rider lost the Working Hunter of the Year title recently with a broken leather buckle when riding the favourite to win. Irons should always be made of stainless steel, as should all bits.

Never buy cheap foreign tack. It will not last, cannot be repaired and looks bad. Best English is far cheaper in the long run.

Never ride in wellingtons with ridges in the sole. If anything goes wrong, particularly while you are jumping, there is a danger of being dragged.

Never ride a horse or pony at a flat-out gallop round corners in rings. Sooner or later you will turn upside down if you do. Most of the top riders have come to grief, myself included at the Royal Show, not even through galloping but simply slipping up on a corner.

Never ride or show a horse or pony while it is coughing. Many people still do, but to the detriment of the horse's future and to its wind.

Never ride, show or hunt a hunter or working-hunter pony with a coloured browband. It is considered very bad etiquette.

Never ride a horse or pony with a sore back or withers. To do so will lead to serious trouble later, and possibly a patch of white hair. Some people are unkind enough to continue riding their animals in this condition without first allowing rest to cure it. To do so often causes the animal to be off sick for some time.

Never ride a horse or pony which you consider stiff or wrong. It may well have azoturia and to continue could be fatal. You must consider your animal's feelings.

Never put rugs or bandages on a young horse or pony for the first time and then leave them. Until familiar with them they will tear them up, much to your frustration.

Never be rude to judges, officials or stewards, no matter how unfair they seem or how badly treated you think you have been. If you feel complaints need to be made, do it in writing to the show director when you get home, explaining the exact circumstances, and he will deal with it correctly.

Never ill-treat, whip or spur a horse at a show, no matter what the circumstances may be. Furthermore the show ring is not a schooling ground – nor is the hunting field.

Never attempt to show a horse or pony that has been operated on in any way for wind or soft palate. To do so will get you and your horse banned from showing.

Never attempt to show a horse or pony that has been pin-fired for curbs or splints.

Never attempt to show or enter a hunter at a qualifying show if not previously registered with the Hunters Improvement Society. To do so will render you ineligible to show that animal for the rest of the season.

Never try to obtain results by using force or gadgets. Improvement can be obtained by patience, care, good animal husbandry and understanding of the aids.

Never work, show or school an animal if in your opinion it is not 100 per cent sound. To do so will render it at risk for future usefulness and permanent damage can so easily be done.

Never fight with your horse or pony. Horsemanship is obtained by using your brains, not brawn.

Never accuse your horse or pony of vice. If it shows unwillingness, its fear or hesitancy is probably due to being in doubt as to your orders.

Never lose your temper when schooling. The old saying, 'If at first you don't succeed, try, try again,' applies to horses in particular. If you persevere over a period of time, you will get the result you require.

Never give too much heating food or oats until the animal is doing sufficient work to warrant it. To do so will only make it unmanageable and difficult to train or show.

Never buy or attempt to ride a horse or pony that is too big and strong or above your natural capabilities. Always seek advice and help from someone with more knowledge than yourself.

Do always make a point of going to see your horse or pony last thing at night to check that all is well. If animals are left from 5pm until 8am next day, much can go wrong. Rugs can slip round, the animal could be cast or have broken out into a sweat after travelling, or could be suffering with colic, to name but a few disasters.

Do always check, prior to entering the show ring, your girth, keepers and bits. Irons and leathers must be large enough to accommodate a tall, big male judge if necessary.

Do always check, on arrival at a show, that your exhibit is entered in the right section and class. It is has been known for a heavyweight hunter to end up in the Welsh section on more than one occasion. If such matters are seen to on arrival, any errors may be corrected, or at least you will not have got yourself and your exhibit ready unnecessarily.

Do always freshly trim up your animal prior to a show. Nothing looks worse than top knots or pieces of mane at the bottom of the neck about an inch long, and half-grown whiskers. It's similar to a man looking as if he needs a shave.

Do always give your animal a pat and try to relax when entering the ring. A tense horse and rider will not win prizes.

Do always remember, if you are not in the position of prize winner and think you should be, that there is always another day, another judge and another show.

Do always remember, if in doubt of show-ring procedure, to ask professional advice. If approached at the right time and place (not just prior to a class and going into the ring), you will find people very helpful. This, of course, applies to all matters concerning the horse.

Do always remember that a judge is not required to give his reasons for class placings. If, after a class, you do happen politely to ask about a certain horse or pony, the judge may well be helpful. On no account should you attack him as to the whys and wherefores. I remember one person asking me why I did not like her animal, to which I replied, 'Madam, it was not that I did not like your exhibit, I just liked the ones in front better'!

Do always remember, when showing champions that have rarely been beaten under many different judges, to retire them gracefully from the show ring when they start either to get beaten regularly by younger animals or go sour. It always seems such a shame when past champions, through no fault of their own, stand down the line.

Do always unplait your exhibit's mane as soon after a class as possible, because if you leave it until you arrive home, you will find that the mane gets very thin after several shows.

Do always at the start of the season or, in fact, if in any doubt about bitting problems, have your horse's teeth examined by an expert.

Do always remember in hot weather to use a fly spray on your exhibit prior to entering the ring or, as some animals dislike sprays, put some on a cloth and wipe him over, especially the legs. Some animals really cannot and will not put up with flies.

Do always remember to dress correctly, not only in the show ring but also in the hunting field and while hacking and schooling. To dress correctly does not necessitate buying everything new. This rule applies equally to tack.

Do always remember that, with care, schooling and overall production, many an ugly duckling has been turned into a swan, and this is particularly true in the case of youngsters. Many past champion horses and ponies have come from the ranks of the unknown, sometimes shown in the wrong classes because of the inexperience of their owners, sometimes unwittingly put up for sale but spotted by experts who were able to appreciate their qualities. I have found champions in fields where they have been bred and in market places. One champion hunter was stabled in a railway carriage in Wales, and another champion small hunter was tied up outside a pub one Sunday as I drove by and later that year won the Royal Show. Finding show horses and ponies in unlikely places adds to the fascination of the show world. It also proves that champions can be found and bought for small money even in this day and age, which gives encouragement to everyone. To own a champion one does not necessarily have to pay thousands of pounds. One does have to acquire what is called an eye for a horse, and many people not only have that eye but can also see a good animal in the rough.

Do always remember to have your animal's vaccination certificate checked by an expert at the start of the season. This particularly applies when buying a new animal. Each year at the Horse of the Year Show and the Royal International, many horses and ponies are sent home, much to the distress of the owners, simply because their certificates are out of date by only a day or two, but rules are rules and are there to be obeyed and not broken.

Do always ensure, when showing hacks and children's ponies, that they are well worked in and quiet prior to entering the ring, as no lapse in manners is allowed in these classes whatsoever. However, hunters are allowed a buck or bout of exuberance under some judges provided that they get on with the job afterwards.

Do always, during the judging of any class, pay attention to the steward's and judge's orders, as many a rosette has been lost through not paying attention.

Do always, when going out to buy an animal for the show ring, take an experienced person with you for guidance and have it vetted well by a horse specialist.

No horse or pony is perfect. Having found what, in your opinion, is good enough starting material, careful production will then help you to achieve the rest. You will not, however, get away with curbs, spavins, ringbones and sidebones or horses or ponies making a noise in their wind. How much you can put up with incorrect limbs, i.e. badly shaped fore legs and hind legs, depends on the standards you set yourself in matters of conformation and on the standard of show you wish to enter.

Appendix
Rules, regulations and useful addresses

British Show Hack, Cob and Riding Horse Association

The objects of this association are to improve the showing and judging standards and to encourage shows to affiliate and abide by rules and regulations. All owners, exhibitors and riders must be members of the association. No rider under the age of fifteen years is eligible to ride a horse at affiliated shows. Once an animal is registered with the general stud book or any other official body, under no circumstances can the name of the horse be changed. At affiliated shows, hacks are barred from entry in riding-horse classes and vice versa at the same show.

The National Light Horse Breeding Society (H.I.S.)

Show Hunter Regulations
RULES AND REGULATIONS
JANUARY 1984
(Reproduced by kind permission)

1. Before a Ridden Show Hunter or Working Hunter is eligible for *entry* in a class which is a qualifying competition for the Horse of the Year Show, it must have been included on the Society's Show Hunter Register for that year and its Show Hunter Registration number quoted on all Show entry forms. The fact that an animal may already be registered in the Hunter Stud Book does not mean that it is exempt from being registered as a Show Hunter as the latter is an annual registration and the certificate issued will only apply to the current season.

2. *Any horse that is entered for a qualifying class without first being on the 1984 Show Hunter Register cannot subsequently be registered and therefore will not be eligible for entry in any qualifying classes for the remainder of the season.*

3. All owners of Show Hunters must be paid up members of the H.I.S. before the registration will be accepted.

4. Show Hunters must be registered in their correct class, *i.e.* Lightweight up to 12 stone 7 pounds; Middleweight 12 stone 7 pounds and not exceeding 14 stone; Heavyweight over 14 stone. If a horse is transferred into a higher weight class by the Judges on more than one occasion, the owner

must inform the Society immediately and the animal's registration will be amended. Owners can appeal against this decision if they think fit, in which case the Society will appoint a referee to give a final decision. If a horse's registered weight class is altered after the closing date of entries for a Show, it must still appear in the class for which it is entered and the revised Registration Certificate shown to the Judge and his permission sought to appear in the higher weight class.

5. Once a Judge has commenced judging a class, a horse or rider may not leave the ring without the permission of the Judge and Ring Steward. Once a class has commenced, there shall be no change of rider, except in a Championship Class, when a competitor finds they have more than one exhibit eligible to compete.

6. No exhibitor may enter and show a horse under a Judge who is known to have bred, sold, produced or received financial gain from that horse (Stud fees exempt from financial gain).

7. When a Show Hunter is sold, the Registration Certificate must be returned to the Secretary of the H.I.S. immediately with the new owner's name and address given on the reverse side. The new owner will then be sent a registration form to enable the horse to be re-registered under the new ownership before it can be shown again in a qualifying class. No change of horse's name allowed during the current show season.

8. The person in whose name the horse is entered will be held responsible for abiding by the Rules and Regulations of the Show concerned and indemnifying it against any claims for damages, etc, which may arise. If a horse changes ownership after the closing date of entries, it must be re-registered in the name of the new owner before it is eligible to be shown, although it may not be possible to change the details printed in the catalogue.

9. In the Lightweight, Middleweight, Heavyweight and Small Hunter Classes, the highest placed horse in each class will qualify to enter at Wembley unless it has already done so, in which case the second horse will go forward. No horse lower than second place will qualify. In the Working Hunter Class the two highest placed horses will qualify to enter at Wembley. No horse lower than second will qualify. When there are two Working Hunter Classes, the first and second prize winners in each class will compete in the championship to determine which two horses will qualify. In the case of horses qualifying at Shows held after 15th August, 1984, the Horse of the Year Show office must have the entry within two days of the date of that Show (Tel. 01–235 6431).

Useful Addresses

British Show Hack, Cob and Riding Horse Association,
British Show Jumping Association,
British Equestrian Federation,
Joint Measurement Society Ltd,
British Horse Society,
are all at the following address:

British Equestrian Centre
Stoneleigh, Kenilworth, Warwickshire

British Show Pony Society
124 Green End Road, Sawtry, Huntingdon, Cambs PE17 5XA

The Sidesaddle Association
The Secretary, Foxworth Farm, Stitchins Hill, Leigh Sinton, Worcs

Hunters Improvement Society and National Light Horse Breeding Society
96 High Street, Edenbridge, Kent TN8 5AR

Index

Page numbers in *italic* refer to illustrations